Kevin Fortuna's complex and compelling characters can't be separated from the equally rich family drama and surprising twists of his narratives, always the sign of a real writer. I'm in awe of this man's imagination and this story collection. A wonderful debut.

—**Joseph Boyden,** Giller Prize-winning author of *The Orenda* and *Through Black Spruce*

These stories are by turns wry and funny, harrowing and heartbreaking. Kevin Fortuna writes with startling clarity and insight about success, hope and longing and about people struggling to do the right thing, and sometimes failing. He writes with his heart and his head and with a sheer ballsy velocity you don't come across very often.

—**Kevin Moffett** , author of *Further Interpretations of Real-Life Events* and *The Silent History*

The Dunning Man is a collection of relentless and often unsettling stories told with intensity and uncommon skill. With clear, exacting prose Kevin Fortuna presents damaged yet indelible characters grappling with shame, pain, and darkness as they teeter on the brink. One gets the sense that these men and women are only hanging on by a thread, and Fortuna triumphs by refusing to let us look away.

—**Skip Horack**, Stegner Fellow and award-winning author of *The Southern Cross* and *The Eden Hunter*.

This muscular collection is inhabited by people whose lives are, as one of them puts it, "pinwheeling out of control." Paralyzed by the past, they can't picture a future beyond the next drink. If you met them in a bar, you would move to the other side of the room. But when you meet them in this book, you'll find yourself frozen in your seat, riveted by their train-wreck tales of heartbreak and (almost) dashed hopes. Thanks to Kevin Fortuna's empathetic and precise portrayals, these stories will linger in your imagination long after the people you meet here have stumbled out into the night.

—**Miles Harvey**, author of *The Island of Lost Maps.*

Kevin Fortuna's people are people written about too little— people on the outskirts, scrapping and scratching, probably not a college degree or reliable job among them. Most often looking for the magic of a big score, as are we all. If they as characters were to be judged by a panel of fictional characters more often seen, the inhabitants of Fortuna's world might be described by the precious characters out there as bleak and hopeless, dirty and depraved, without prospects, out of place in the world, sad. That's why I don't read fiction about precious characters. Fortuna's people defy life by living, and suck every last breath out of a deflated balloon. They are exhilarating people with fully lived lives, expertly drawn. Fortuna's people are people you'd want to know, whose lives you may well admire. They may even be you.

—**Mark Warren**, Executive Editor of *Esquire* magazine.

THE
DUNNING MAN

KEVIN FORTUNA

Lavender Ink
New Orleans
lavenderink.org

The Dunning Man

Published in New Orleans by Lavender Ink.

This is a work of fiction. Any resemblance between the characters presented here and real people is purely coincidental.

ISBN: 978-1935084-64-8

Other editions:
Cloth: 978-1-935084-63-1
Ebook: 978-1935084-65-5

Cover Design: Natalie Slocum
Book design: Bill Lavender

ACKNOWLEDGEMENTS

I would like to thank the following people who provided invaluable help and inspiration in the making of of this book: Joseph and Amanda Boyden, Bill Lavender, Rev. James P. Walsh, S.J., Heather Schroder, John Kenney, Mark Warren, Tim Farley, Michael Clayton, and my two brothers, Joey and Harry Fortuna. Lastly, I would like to thank Fiona, without whom I could never have written these pages.

THE DUNNING MAN

THE
DUNNING MAN

Tá an leabhar seo tiomnaithe do Jack Durcan.

This book is dedicated to Jack Durcan.

DEAD

I come through the side door of Port Authority that leads to the casino buses. I'm running late. Rush hour starts at four o'clock, and missing the three-thirty bus means I'd hit North Jersey traffic and be late for my date with Ursula. Being late would snuff out whatever flame still flickers between us. Can't happen. We've made it this far, and I've done so much planning for tonight that my brain aches. Planned it all down to the last penny.

I move away from the stampede, stuff a piece of nicotine gum between my front lip and my gum like chaw, orient myself.

I board the down escalator. I'm scared. I'm excited. It's not just about the date with Ursula. Coming to this place always gives me the same sense of doom and possibility. This great, crumbling transit dungeon, full of the poison smell of bus exhaust and the swarms of people hurling themselves at dark underground portals to nowhere. My gate is Number 1, the farthest of the Academy gates, and I have less than ten minutes to get there. Getting off the escalator, I am cut off by a short, thick Latina mother dragging an impossible number of suitcases and shopping bags behind her, plus four small kids. What the fuck? How about a little awareness of your surroundings, señora? But then she smiles at me, radiating warmth and goodness. Just look at her and her kids. Don't be an asshole. *Lo siento, mamacita.* The smallest of her children is a wobbly little jammer wearing a stuffed-animal monkey backpack with a monkey tail that doubles as a leash and tethers him to mama. The monkey's head is precisely the size of the boy's head, and level with it, and both faces are grinning as if connected by a Siamese brain stem. The boy's eyelids are pinned wide open with rapture, and I believe he's the happiest human I've seen in months. His little teeth are perfect. I look back up at his saint of a mother and return her smile and get the urge to climb inside the harness of my own monkey backpack and be led around by her. So cozy.

The nicotine has hit my bloodstream and reminds me why I quit the stuff. I'm flying. I love all these people. I'll make my bus. Ursula and I will be fine.

Then I see a twenty-something brunette, pretty as the lobby bar at the Soho Grand, pointing her nose up and away toward a bus that will take her to a better place. She's got a backpack, too, but it's of the tiny black leather variety, probably bought at one of the couture shops deep in the Meatpacking District, an expensive announcement of the tyranny she wields over the males of the species. More powerful than mace. She swishes by me, dismissing me with a flick of her eyes that reminds me of Ursula. An Ursula-in-Training, she is. Shouldn't you already be riding in style to Amagansett, honey? Shouldn't you be sipping some kind of berry-and-vitamin-infused mineral water, your perfect bum nestled in a plush reclining seat? Why steerage class for you today, miss? Daddy's Porsche in the shop? Jitney sold out? Her hair is thick and shiny and jet-black, pulled tight into a ponytail, a curtain opened up to reveal the holy geometry on top of her neck. I permit myself to follow her for a few steps, using up precious time I don't have and wondering where she's going, where she's been, and whether she's ever had a problem bigger than a split end. She wears a formfitting black dress that stops just above the middle of her thighs and shows off her angrily perfect curves. No small effort to keep up what she's got going on there. Perfection wields its own tyranny.

A guy, some kind of construction worker with a dirty face and a hard hat and an oil can of Budweiser in his hand, walks toward us, and I see Ursula-in-Training give him a much different kind of look, an eye-locking "maybe-I'd-let-you-do-me" look. Then she catches herself and laughs and walks faster. Oh, kids.

I hate all these people, these lost souls.

I stop following her. I've got my own Amagansett. Ursula awaits. Can't linger. Casino bus leaves for Atlantic City in four and a half minutes, and I need to get all the way to Gate 1, get my ticket, and get into proper seat-blocking position. I'm screwed. I break into a run, a sprint. I need to catch this bus. I'm out of breath and maybe out of time. The line for tickets is mercifully short, but the ticket-holder line for the bus is long, maybe too long for me to get a seat. Just as I'm about to take up my place in line, a fight starts brewing. A huge woman in a floral-print smock stomps by me and starts asking loudly where the line ends. Her dyed-blonde hair looks like it hasn't been washed in a year, and she has the zombie-eyed look of a junkie. She just about kills the little octogenarian guy walking up behind me. She sumo-bounces him with the widest part of her girth, knocks him off balance, and almost somersaults him over his walker before he regains his balance. "Fuck you, fatty," he says to her. Right on, pappy. The woman turns to him, killing in her eyes, but when he doesn't flinch, she seems to realize her disadvantage. She starts searching for other prey.

Luckily she spots her boyfriend or husband in the crowd. She yells at him, "Bo, where the hell have you been? I've been looking all over. You idiot. You fucking moron. Come *here*. *Now*."

He pretends not to see her, though every single person on line is staring at her. It's going to be a long bus ride. Time for the real thing. I take a tin of chaw out of my pocket, scoop the nicotine gum from my lip, and replace it with a heap of Skoal Long Cut Wintergreen. That's the medicine.

"Bo, get your dumb ass over here *now*!"

"I'm coming," he says, not making eye contact, not daring to peel his eyes off the floor. For the first time I see that there might be something wrong with him—mentally. Keeping his head down, he moves toward her, and as soon as he's close enough, she reaches up and grabs a fistful of his hair in one hand, holds his head steady, and slaps him so hard with the other hand that the whole line goes quiet. The violence is swift and confident, an old habit between them. Someone else says, "Damn, girl!" Fatty doesn't come out of her trance. She's still got a grip on his hair and she's twisted his head down so she can whisper something in his ear. He looks like he might cry. He takes it, doesn't try to pull away. She slaps him again, lightly this time, almost lovingly, and then finally lets him go.

He straightens himself out, shakes his head, and looks her in the eyes for the first time. "We're done," he says. "I'm leaving you. We're done."

"Oh, no we're not. Shut your filthy goddamn mouth and give me those bus tickets."

She didn't have to ask. He's already fishing them out of his pocket. He pulls two tickets out and hands her one, and then he turns around and walks away without another word.

Good for him. Maybe he *is* done. Now the bus ride will be

much quieter. The driver stands at the head of the line, counting us up. He walks the line and counts us three times. Then he gets on his radio and calls for another bus. He turns to us and announces that some people won't get seats, but that another bus will pick up the rest of us within an hour. He starts boarding people. This'll take a while. I've seen it before. People go to the bathroom or reach under their seats and don't get counted, and the driver needs to start all over again. I turn to the old guy with the walker and ask him to hold my spot, then I walk out beside the bus to a little cluster of smokers with the same purpose as me. I fish in my pocket and bring out the half pack of American Spirits I'd been hoarding for this trip. I shake one out and get a light off a young black guy wearing a Yankee cap with the tags still on. He fires himself up a Newport in solidarity. "She a crazy bitch, right?" he says. I just nod, my head a million miles away, imagining the reckoning I'll face if I'm late for Ursula.

The driver steps off the bus and announces in a flat tone that he's only got six more seats. I count up the spots in front of me and see that I am one of the six, the next to last one. I take a long drag off my cigarette, carefully put it out, and put the rest of it back in the pack for later. Just as I start to head back inside, I see Fatty's beaten-down boy, Bo, walk up and take up his place in line with her like nothing ever happened. I see the old man screw up his face and start yelling at them and trying to get the driver's attention. Fatty and Bo ignore him. So does the driver. The old man looks at me like a drowning man looking for air. It's him or me. I nod at him and point toward the bus door, telling him he should board. I take my unfinished cigarette out of my pack and bum another light off the black kid.

17

While walking the six short and two long blocks from Port Authority to Penn Station, I tell myself I am different from these bus people. I have a job, and a profession to which I will eventually return. I've eaten in five-star restaurants. I've slept with a Lands' End model—twice. I will take the train, by God, because I am too good for these people that ride the casino buses from Port Authority. It will be tight but I'll survive without my slot-machine coupon. I'll win back the difference at the tables, or skimp on something that Ursula won't notice. The train is so much more civilized. It will calm me down and put me in the correct frame of mind for the night. Plus, no traffic, so no risk of being late for Ursula. Should've planned it this way from the beginning.

Penn Station feels like the Louvre to me after Port Authority. Just look at the flipping letters and numbers on the board. Old school. Look at the Zaro's, and the people in suits and dresses. High heels, not flats. Trains, not buses. This is my world. The Amtrak ticket kiosk asks me if I want to upgrade to a first-class seat for twenty-five dollars more, and I do it. Why not? I'm worth it. Not a frugal move, but tonight's not the night for being cheap. It's the night of make it happen. I find a bathroom and lock myself in a stall. I reach into my pocket and pull out my little bag of tricks. Ziploc'd for freshness. I need to plan, so A is my man. A is for Adderall, A is for amphetamine. A is for cerebral cortex in pill form. Hot damn.

First class, baby, upstairs in the red seats where the fancy people ride, where they hand out menus and mixed drinks. Ketel One and soda, thank you very much. Go heavy on the pour, garçon, more, more, more… that's it, there she blows. Nice execution. I'd tip you more than a dollar for that there pour, but I'm already

18

fifty-six dollars over budget. Speaking of, I need a four-seater to do my work. There's an empty one, at the far end of the car, that's got my name on it. Look at the high-end peeps in this joint, dude right there with a tuxedo on. Let me get my Ketel on and might need to have a chat with him, see what's up. Then there's the huge Italian bloke who's balding and will be wearing a hairpiece in a matter of months. Atlantic City is his stomping ground, methinks, so he is probably a force to be reckoned with. To my right are some Arabs, and you know they got it going on, they got the harems, the mad paper. No Fattys or Bos around here.

Whoa. Hold up. There she is. Look at her. Earth angel... I'm in love—completely, madly in love, times two (haven't forgotten you, U). No time for losers, her nose in a book, and what a beautiful nose it is. Behold the perturbed way she holds her book, bending its cover as if it will change the story she's reading. She cares about whatever is in those pages. She cares about the world. About Elvis. She's an animal lover but shaves her legs and doesn't wear patchouli oil. Just look at her. She is my reason for being. Gives me hope for life after death. Can't talk to her yet, though, gotta get set up.

Drop my stuff on the four-seater and push on to the other side of the car to find the bathroom. The train is moving now, and the noise makes a difference. Motion, progress. Rattles my bones, makes the whole thing real somehow. Going to see my girl. Ursula, the Queen. The Girlbomb. The Unattainable. Save me, Ketel. Help me survive. I know, I know, you'll do what you can but it's not enough. Head spinning too fast now. Need a painkiller. Into the bathroom and out of my pocket comes the bag o' tricks. Ziploc'd for freshness. I need to chill, so V is my pill. V is for Vicodin. V is for vacuum up the Adderall, calm me down. Wash her down, Ketel.

Back to my four-seater. I extend the tray tables and empty out my pockets onto them and sit down. There before me against the stark whiteness of the tables is all the gas I have for cooking. Less than a quarter tank. Three hundred-dollar bills, a fifty, and four twenties. I have two hundred dollars more on my debit, but need to leave it for incidentals at the Chelsea, the hotel I picked. Couldn't rent the room without it and it cost me five phone calls to the head manager to get it done. He obviously didn't understand how busy I am. And, of course, my lucky deck of cards, in case of a true emergency. All in the service of U. U is for unattainable. U is for Ursula. U is for un-fucking-believable how gorgeous that girl is four rows up. Those fingers of hers, the frizz of her hair lit up by the sunlight streaking through the windows. Her perfect getaway sticks, curled up beneath her behind. And what a behind it is. I can see it because it rests on her heels and she leans sideways and her painted-on jeans don't leave much to the imagination. She looks up from her book and the laser beams that are her eyes lock onto mine and I turn to pudding. Oh, kids. No fair. You're not Ursula. You're not the Queen. If I had a wedding ring, I'd be twisting it. If I had game, I'd be using it. If I had a beer, I'd be drinking it. I see a waitress just in time. Nurse, give me a Miller Lite and make me remember high school, please. Thank you, my dear. As I take the beer from her, she leans over, points with a flick of her eyes at the Johnny Three Chins, and whispers this warning: "Be careful around that one. I saw him almost kill a guy on this train once. Smashed his face in. Cops came but didn't even arrest him." The warning is wasted on me.

What do I care? I'm an hour on this train now, which means I'm nearly halfway home, halfway to U is for Unbelievable. So there is the cooking gas, and I'm short and there's no denying it. I can get drinks and dinner tonight, maybe, but that will tap me out. So funny. Once upon a time my money flowed like wine, and a night like this was as easy as sneezing. That's when Miss U couldn't get enough of my confections. I'd be slinging mortgages and CDOs and everyone be gettin' out of my way. That's what I'm talking about. That's the thing about it.

So the shortage will just need to be solved, like all things. It won't stand in the way of fate. Speaking of, look at that paisan, fat and alone, but so sure of what he is not, what he left alone when he was three. Just look at him, his guayabera, his pinkie ring, his big silver cross chained to his neck. Awesome. Even his red, fleshy earlobes contain pent-up fury. Come on, now. He's some mother's son, he got choked up when he watched *ET.* He needs a friend. I stand up, feel my lucky cards in my pocket, and move toward him, not knowing why, not knowing what will happen. Next thing I know I'm sitting next to him, invading his space.

"What do you need?" he asks me.

"Nothing," I say. "Sorry. I'm bored and a little drunk and was hoping you'd tell me what to do when I get to Atlantic City."

"Turn around and leave," he says, and then he smiles and laughs and then coughs a deep, wheezy cough.

"Are you from there?"

"Born and bred."

"I'm Connor." I stick out my hand, and he reaches out a big meaty paw to grab it. He smiles warmly and seems in that moment to stop hating me for disturbing me. I notice the fishhook tattoo

21

on his neck and the Rolex on his wrist.

"What do you do, Connor?"

"Wish I knew. Kind of finding my way. Had a semblance of a career before the markets crashed, but… guess I'm rebuilding now, so to speak."

"Are you gay?"

"Come again?"

"Are you a faggot, Connor?"

"No. Why?"

"Just have to ask. Gating question. We're on a train to Atlantic City, where anything goes. You walked up to me and sat down and started talking to me. And I don't know you from Adam."

"Fair enough. I'm actually heading down to AC to try to patch things up with the love of my life."

"Love of your life? What are you, fifteen? Can you even drive a car, Connor?"

"Just about to be middle-aged. I'll be thirty in three weeks."

"And you love this girl, do you?"

I swallow hard. He looks at me with all his Italian bullshit, the swirl of his dark eyes and the knowing way his fat self spills into the seat next to him. "Yeah, I suppose I do love her. Never known anything like it. Can't help it."

"Good for you. Hold on to it. Lightning doesn't usually strike twice."

"Really?"

He turns away, coughs. Some kind of meanness passes over him. He doesn't answer.

Without knowing why, I ask him, "Where do you want to be in ten years?"

"Dead."

We're both quiet for a bit. I think about asking him why he wants to be dead, but I don't have the faintest dumb urge to pull out my lucky cards on him. Instead I get up and move back toward my four-seater. I'm wobbly, drunk, and staggered by the V is for Vicodin. I should really sleep it off before reaching back into my bag o' tricks. I recline my seat and pass out.

I wake up to an announcement from the conductor. The train is stopped, some kind of mechanical issue. We're deep into the Pine Barrens, the fetid wilderness of South Jersey. The sun is setting. My cell phone is blinking at me. A text from Ursula. She's tied up and doesn't want to meet tonight. She wants to know if we can meet tomorrow night instead. It's beyond her control, she says. She's sorry. She really is. And I can hear the lilt of her voice in the words on my cell phone. I can feel the breath that comes out of her mouth when she speaks them. God, she's so beautiful, so rarefied. So lost to me.

I need air. I stand up and move toward the back of the car, wondering if there's a way to stand between the cars. I see that perfect girl with that perfect behind and her nose in the books, still reading. She looks up at me, holds my eyes for a moment, and looks back at her book. I keep moving toward the door.

WEDDINGS AND BURIALS

The Irish had come over in full force for the latest Fahey wedding. When I got to the reception, Dee Dougherty and her sister-in-law Anne Fahey were huddled in front of one of the floor-to-ceiling windows overlooking the cemetery, sipping from clear plastic cups of white wine and whispering to each other about my husband. They stood with their backs toward me. I'd just fetched my own chardonnay from the nearby bar, and was heading toward them to say hello when I overheard them.

"That's it? That's where he did it?" Anne said.

"Yes—over there, in the fourth row. The Linden grave. It has cameras on it now, and you can see the little security sign."

"Imagine such a thing. Jesus. Jesus in holy heaven."

When Dee Dougherty said "Jesus" with her Cork accent, it sounded like "Jay-zuhss." Like some kind of drunken banshee. She always was a loud one, and she liked her wine. I circled around them and saw them before they noticed me. Anne had a warm, kind smile on her face—which was still quite beautiful despite her more than sixty years. Her straight gray hair pulled back in a tight bun, those Audrey Hepburn cheekbones, that itsy pinky of a nose, those teeth lined up perfectly like a row of tiny white bricks—it all still did the trick for her. She'd always been a great beauty. I couldn't blame Eddie for picking Anne back in Cobh, when we were all just kids. As he put it, Anne got the face and I got the personality, and he was a face man. True enough. I could make the boys laugh like I was one of them. Brian used to tell me to stop being so funny, that it wasn't right that I was so much funnier than him. Women shouldn't be so funny, he'd say. Oh, Brian. What a fool thing to say.

So there I was, frozen in place, thinking about the harsh truth of Eddie's choice, trying to decide if I should veer off or go talk to the Fahey sisters as I'd planned. Fuck it, I thought. Coming here, I knew there'd be jokes and sly looks and clucking tongues, and I promised myself I wouldn't let any of it get to me. I took a swig from my glass, put my head down, and walked toward Dee and Anne, bracing myself for the jolt of embarrassment they'd feel when they saw me.

Dee saw me first and hugged me like she meant it, a little too fast and rough. "Oh, look who it is! Our little Rosie!"

Anne pulled me to her and air-kissed me, but her smile seemed genuine and never left her face when she saw me. "Rosie, you never get older," she said. "You don't look a day older than forty."

"She *is* like a bottle of fine wine that gets better with age," Dee spat, before tossing back what was left in her cup. A splash of wine missed her mouth and streaked across her cheek, glistening with reflected light from the chandelier above us. She couldn't feel it through her thick makeup, but it was all I could see while she blathered on. "What is your secret, Rosie? Wheat germ? Fish oil? Or is it one of those exotic fruits everyone is raving about now? Do you know the ones? Pomegranate. Kiwi. Cactus, maybe? Some Yank on the plane over talked Eddie's ear off about something called a Nonni. From Tahiti or someplace like that. Swore it cures cancer, stops the flu, destroys fat, and builds muscle. On and on. Talked about it like it's the bloody fountain of youth. He was a salesman for it, and tried to tell Eddie he should be one, too—*ha! imagine! Eddie!* Anyway, we got stuck on the tarmac at Shannon for an hour with some kind of mechanical problem and Eddie had his fill of the Yank and his Nonni, so at one point he says to your man, 'Look. Why don't you bring yourself and some of that magic Nonni potion up to the pilot, so he can pour it in the tank of this bloody plane and get us on our way?'"

We all had a laugh about Eddie taking the piss out of the Yank. I could just see him saying it, with the whiskey in his hand, the crafty smile on his face. I considered telling Dee about the droplet of wine on her face but decided against it.

"Now where's your Brian?" Dee asked. Her eyebrows scrunched with charmless curiosity.

"Oh, he's around here somewhere."

"Well, I need to say howdy. Haven't seen his handsome face yet. How's his work?"

"Good, good," I said. Brian hadn't had any kind of real job since being fired from this place, and Dee knew it full well. "I need a refill. What about you girls?"

Anne and Dee nodded, and I took their empty cups and headed toward the bar. As I walked away from them, the air on my face felt like freedom, and I started to unclench. Wouldn't it have been nice if someone slipped a little something in Dee's cup of wine? Nothing too crazy or dangerous. Maybe one of those party pills the kids had been talking about—a roofie or whatever they call it. Just something to put her over the edge, make her wobbly enough to lose her legs a time or two before the end of the night. I'd do it if I had one in my purse. I had some Paxil, but that would probably just make her more alert and happy. That wouldn't do. Maybe if I crushed up six or seven pills and put them in her drink it would get her. But no. The thought of it made me smile. But that was more the chardonnay talking than anything else. Chardonnay was my best friend right now, and I couldn't wait to have another. I got in line at the bar behind a bunch of strange young faces. Friends of the bride and groom, in a hurry to get drunk. My own children couldn't be here, or so they said. I knew better.

Now, I'm no great defender of my husband, but I do think if another man had done it—if, say, Eddie Fahey had done it— somehow it would have been turned into a funny stunt, or even a bit of delayed justice. A feather in his cap. But not so with Brian. Brian got crucified for it, and they still hadn't let him come down off his cross. Everyone asked why he did it, but it has always been pretty plain to me. He felt trapped and figured it would do no harm if nobody found him out. Figured he could get away with it. He'd been getting away with things all his life. The lifelong teamster pension that followed the Irish-football injury just before his twenty-sixth birthday, the girls he had before—and probably after—meeting me. Part of it was chance. Part of it was his good looks. (When we were vacationing in Los Angeles one time, he won a James Dean look-alike contest and we drank for free the whole night.) God knows it wasn't his personality, which had kept him unemployed and isolated for years. He couldn't get along with his own children, even now that they were grown. Brian got the face all right, but Eddie got the balls and heart and sense of humor.

The gambling debts had gotten out of hand, Brian said after he got caught. And he had gotten into debt with some brutal men who had threatened to harm me and the children. I can still remember the day he called me from this place in a panic.

The cops were on to him, he kept saying. He was heaving and whimpering like a child. When I finally got him to calm down enough to make sense, he told me what he'd done as if confessing it in church. Later came his rationalization. Linden was a Nazi and the watch was contraband from the war. The family came to eat at the Natchez after the funeral, and that's how he found out about it. They'd tried for years to find the watch's rightful owners, who they suspected were prisoners at Auschwitz. The old man wanted to do the right thing in the end, and so did the family. Apparently the watch was a rare Rolex, one of the first ever made, and was worth more than $30,000. What got Brian in the end were his fingerprints on the axe that he used to finish the job on the grave's padlock.

Disgusted by the memory, and the shame and ruin that followed it, I decided to take a break before rejoining Anne and Dee. I got one wine refill instead of the three and headed to the far side of the banquet room, toward a hidden patio I knew about from the old days.

It took me back, being there. Back then, the Natchez Club felt like the world we'd never be part of, the world of the old people whose houses I cleaned. And this enormous banquet room seemed like a Cinderella dream. With its twenty-foot ceilings, dark wood floors, massive chandeliers, white tablecloths, and views of the cemetery and Garden District mansions. I remembered when Brian first got the job more than a decade ago. One of the Fahey cousins from our county owned a big interest in the Natchez, and he knew Brian had been a cook and barman back in Ireland. He gave him a chance, even though he resented him from their time playing football together. Probably on Eddie's say-so, born of some misguided feelings of guilt or regret about me, he made Brian the assistant general manager.

I had such hope for the future then, for a brief time. I never deluded myself to think that Brian would suddenly become the dream husband—after all, we'd been living pretty separate lives for years. But I did think he might've found a job he could keep for a while, and that maybe I wouldn't have to keep cleaning rich people's houses and offices at night to put the kids through college. A better life seemed possible. I imagined first communions and confirmations and graduations and the girls getting married here in this banquet room. Thinking about it now was pure silliness, though. It was too good to be true, and the unreality of it made me wonder from the start when Brian would find a way to fuck it all up. But I'd let myself hope against reason that it could last. And I guess I didn't expect him to blow up in such spectacular fashion.

I walked out a side door of the ballroom. I needed to be alone for a few minutes more. I needed to finish this cup of wine and clear my head before going back to the reception. I went past the ladies' room, took a right, and found the small patio off the kitchen. Good. None of the smokers had found it yet. The sun had set. The patio was unlit and stood some distance from the ballroom, but I could see the wedding party through the ballroom's big windows. I could see the wedding people but they couldn't see me. The newlyweds had been summoned for their first dance and they were moving around, to and fro, eyes locked on each other, self-conscious smiles on their faces. They looked positively miserable. Poor things. If they thought this was bad, wait till they saw what they'd let themselves in for. I thought of the other couples I'd seen dance on that same floor over the years, at the wedding receptions held at the Natchez when Brian still worked here, and at the other family weddings of the Fahey kids and two of the Moran family kids. Brian stopped coming to family events after he lost his job here, but I kept coming, maybe out of spite. Right here on this very patio, at Lucy Moran's wedding, only a little more than a year after his brother fired Brian, Eddie Fahey invited me out here for a smoke and professed his love, drunk as a priest. I could still remember his red eyes and his unsteady voice. The sadness of it. The exhilaration of being wanted like that again. The way he grabbed me and pressed up against me, like he was doing his best imitation of a movie star. The whiskey on his breath. The touch of his coarse, stubby carpenter's fingers, like big nail files scraping across my face and neck when he kissed me.

"Hello, Ms. Casey," a man said behind me.

Startled, I turned around and saw old Rodney Meeks, the club's handyman, sitting in a dark corner of the patio, smoking one of his trademark menthol cigarettes.

"My God. Rodney? Rodney Meeks? Is that you?"

"Yes, ma'am. In the flesh."

"Well, you're a sight for sore eyes," I said, still shaking from the fright he gave me.

"Nice to see you, too, Ms. Casey."

Funny how Rodney always addressed me as "Ms." instead of "Mrs." I used to wonder if it was a subtle dig against Brian. All these years later and Rodney still worked here. Amazing. I always loved Rodney Meeks. He had a kind of stoic wisdom. He always seemed glad to see me.

Brian and he didn't get along too well, from what I remembered. It had something to do with the fact that Rodney once upstaged him in front of the kitchen staff by lighting the gas pilot on a stove that Brian had struggled for hours to fix before proclaiming it broken and dead.

"Nice day for a party," he said.

"It is, indeed."

"So it's the old man Fahey's granddaughter getting married?"

"Yes."

"She sure is pretty."

"Yes. She got the Fahey looks."

Suddenly I wondered what Rodney knew. I wondered if he knew the whole story about Brian. I wondered, irrationally, if he knew about me and Eddie, if he could see the memory of our kiss that had just left my head.

"How have you been, Rodney?"

"I can't complain. An' nobody would care if I did. My health is okay. Doctor said I should quit the cigarettes, but I can't see how it makes much difference now. I only got so much time left anyhow. Only so many more weddings and burials before my own time comes. Figure I might as well enjoy what's left."

"How's your family, Rodney? How's your wife?"

"Betsy's been gone now about five years, Ms. Casey. But my boys are good. Both in college now."

"Oh, Rodney. I'm sorry. I'm so sorry about Betsy."

He nodded and looked down and we were both quiet for a few seconds. Then he raised something to his lips—a silver flask. He took a long sip from it. He saw me following it with my eyes, which locked with his for a moment, and then he lowered the flask from his lips and passed it to me in one smooth motion. I drank from it and the cheap whiskey filled my sinuses and warmed the back of my neck. I passed it back to Rodney and thanked him and we watched the people dance on the other side of the glass as if they wouldn't see tomorrow.

"Let me ask you something, Rodney. Now that all this time has gone by. What happened with Brian and that Rogers girl? Why did she tell the Faheys what happened, and how did she know about it in the first place?"

"Been a long time. Let me see what I remember. Armando and Brian planned the thing with the grave. I suppose you know all about that. What you might not know is that I was his lookout boy. . . ." He smiled and shook his head. He took a drag from his smoke and leaned back in his seat. I got the sense that he felt he might've said too much.

"Rodney, you don't need to worry," I said. "This is ancient history. All is forgiven. In fact, Brian's here tonight."

Rodney's eyes widened. "He is? Well, I'll be. Guess time heals, like they say. Anyhow, yeah. So I was moonlighting back then as a neighborhood security guard, so I made sure nobody bothered us while we did the deed. . . . Brian paid me five hundred bucks to do it, which was a lot of money for me then. Yep, sure was. I'm not sorry. I needed the cash. But I didn't bargain for the job we had in front of us. Had I known, I wouldn't've done it for five *thousand* dollars. The night we did it he waited and waited until the streets emptied out. Then he called us and we met at the club, must've been four in the morning. Brian had already done the job with bolt cutters and the axe, but he wanted us to watch the edges of the cemetery for him while he got the watch off the dead man. And everything was fine for a few weeks until the Rogers girl did what she did. Armando told her what happened, because he wanted to get in her pants. Hell, Ms. Casey, *I* wanted to get in her pants, too." I laughed at that, which encouraged Rodney. The whiskey had gone to my head. "Every damn man in this club did. She was *that* pretty. Not nice, you understand, but real good-looking and saucy. Anyhow, the Rogers girl told on Brian because she tried to blackmail him and it didn't work. She wanted half the money to stay quiet, and he refused. So then she threatened to sue and started running her mouth. She claimed Brian was harassing her…" Rodney paused to see how I'd react. I didn't say anything, and he kept going: "…or some nonsense like that. I never liked her, to tell the truth. Never trusted her. But I can't really say what happened for real and what was made up, Ms. Casey. Sure caused a lot of trouble around here till old man Fahey paid her off. She tipped them off about the axe, and once they found it in the crypt, it was over. Damn shame, really, since police in this town couldn't be bothered to look at it too deep. Had to have their work done for them. Linden was a bad man, after all. Some kind of Nazi. She should have just left it alone. But that's life. That's just life."

"Yes, that's just life," I said. Then I took the last sip of my wine. "Why leave the axe, Rodney? Why not burn it or throw it in the river?"

"Have always asked myself the same question. Guess we just left it there in a panic."

We both had a laugh about the axe.

"Thanks, Rodney. It was really good seeing you. Take care of yourself."

"Ms. Casey, there's one more thing. Do me a favor. Tell Brian thank you for me, would you?"

"For what?"

"Well, the way I see it, I owe him a lot. I'm still here at the Natchez because of him. He took the blame for the whole thing. Covered for Armando and me both, and I've never gotten the chance to properly thank him. He told old man Fahey that he made us help him by threatening to fire us. He really did right by us."

"Oh," I said. My cheeks burned, and for a moment I couldn't think or speak. "Well, Rodney, Brian is right out there in the dining room. No reason you can't tell him thank you yourself. I know it would mean a lot to him."

Rodney lowered his eyes and shook his head.

"Okay, Rodney. I'll tell him."

When I went back in, people were fanning out to find their assigned tables. To my surprise, Brian and I were seated at table five, the same table as Eddie and Anne Fahey. Who assigned the seating? Oh, Lord. I made my way over slowly, scanning the crowd for Brian.

"There she is!" said Eddie, standing up to greet me when I reached our table. "How have you been, Mrs. Casey?" He gave me a tight, lingering hug. He held me too long and I let him do it. My head rested on his shoulder for a second and my eyes found Brian walking toward our table, watching us embrace. I wondered what he was thinking—and what Anne was thinking. Brian stopped where he was, about twenty feet away. He stared at me intensely, looking angry, defeated, and somehow satisfied all at once. I felt Eddie wrapped around me still. He was on his way to being drunk. I could smell the whiskey on his breath, and I could hear the raspy sound of him breathing. I remembered the sweet poison taste of his mouth when we kissed, the whiskey and tobacco. I let go, pulled away from Eddie, and sat down. I only turned my head for a second, just long enough to find my seat beneath me. But when I looked back, Brian was gone. I scanned the room but didn't see him. I wondered if he'd left.

For a few minutes, it was just me and the Faheys at the table. To keep things light, I asked Eddie about the Nonni juice and he told us the whole story of getting buttonholed by the American salesman on the plane from Shannon. The story was much funnier coming from Eddie. He had Anne and me laughing.

A few minutes later, the table had filled up. A few minutes after that, Brian finally came and sat down with us. Everyone was polite, but I could tell Brian wanted to disappear.

Eddie didn't make eye contact with him until the dessert came. Then he raised his knife and clinked it against his wineglass to silence the table. "I'd like to raise a glass to the lovely bride and groom, my niece and new nephew-in-law. May they live long lives together and make lots of babies. Hear, hear!"

Everyone raised their glasses and toasted the bride and groom. Then they started talking among themselves again, thinking Eddie had finished his toast. But he hadn't. He tapped his wineglass again, and the table fell silent a second time. "I'd also like to make a toast to someone who is making a homecoming of sorts. Mr. Brian Casey, who used to work for this fine establishment. He stayed away for a while, but he's finally come back to bury the hatchet."

Someone laughed. I don't know who. The hair on the back of my neck stood up. My face flushed. I looked at Brian, who was looking down at his untouched dessert plate. He looked stricken and suddenly old, and my heart went out to him in that moment.

I reached out and took his hand in mine. Without thinking, I stood up and led him onto the dance floor.

For a while, we were the only ones dancing. We danced slowly and did not speak. By the second song, the dance floor had filled up around us. We danced and danced for what seemed like hours. I can remember Eddie and Anne dancing right next to us, and I can remember Anne looking at me with an apology in her eyes. All beauty and grace. I can remember slow dancing with Brian to "Unchained Melody." I can remember trying to imagine what went through Brian's head the night he robbed the dead man. I could picture him skulking about that creepy cemetery, struggling with the wire cutters, drenching his clothes with sweat and constantly wiping it away from his eyes. I could see him cursing and groping through the darkness of the vault and having words with the men who helped him, talking down to them, and them hating him for keeping them there. It must've taken them at least an hour to do it all. What drove him? Were the gambling debts real? Did he do it to just get one over on Eddie? Or did he do it for me? The possibility that he had some kind of a noble purpose, however twisted, had never occurred to me until this moment. Maybe he needed to assert himself. Everyone had gone out and made their way in the world, but, for reasons he would never understand, Brian got left behind, stunted, working for the brother of a man who had scorned his wife back in Ireland.

Funny how Brian's mind filed the event. Long after it happened, he told me that nobody understood. People said he dug up a corpse, but that wasn't true. New Orleans is a swamp, so bodies are buried aboveground, in vaults and crypts, to prevent the coffins from floating away. Cities of the Dead, they call the cemeteries.

He did no digging—just busted a lock to take a stolen watch off a once-evil man. And he planned to give some of the money to charity, some kind of Holocaust museum or something. Nobody understood poor Brian's true intentions.

At one point, they started playing the old songs, and the women started step dancing. A few songs into it, they played an old rebel ballad called "Kitty," about a man who runs away and abandons his lover to escape prison. Before the first verse was sung, Eddie came over and poked Brian on his shoulder, hard. It was more of a shove than a poke, and I could feel the weight of it. "I'll have this next dance with your beautiful bride," he said. It wasn't a request.

I could feel Brian's heartbeat quicken with rage, and it scared me. He let go of me and tried to move away. But I held on to him and leaned forward and put my mouth up to his ear and whispered, "Wait. Please stay." Then I turned to Eddie, met his eyes, and said, "No, Eddie. I don't think so. Not now."

Brian and I finished that dance together. Then, before the next song started, we walked off the dance floor. With our backs turned to the Faheys, we kept walking arm-in-arm and left for home without saying goodbye to anyone.

SULLAPALOOZA

You drive down the winding two-lane road of Hyde Park, past all the mink and manure, the rich and poor, the giant houses built with Wall Street and *Mayflower* money and the trailer park nobody can get rid of. Past the opening of the long tree tunnel that led you to the group home where that black retard shared his joint with you last summer after you wrecked your new truck into a giant oak tree and wandered in the woods for hours. You thought you'd die there, abandoned, until that black boy found you and put his hand on your shoulder and asked you why you were crying. That *hand. Resting. Lightly.* Like he knew all about you. Like some kind of dope-smoking angel of mercy.

Carnage. Trouble. You roll down your window and you can smell it in the cold, wet, dirt-soaked air.

You start down your little brother's driveway and the first thing you see is a flipped-over car in his front yard, one of its wheels spinning and flames shooting up from behind it. It takes you a few seconds to believe your eyes, but that *is for goddamn sure what it is.* Big ol' Cadillac. Black and long, banged-up to hell, one of its huge doors open to show its cream-colored seats, and the fire rising behind it. Could be that '78 Sully kept out back, up on blocks. You wonder how it got here. How he made it happen.

Truck and tractor parts are scattered all over the yard. The tailpipe, the radiator, and what looks like an engine block from an 18-wheeler. And your brother's house, the blue rain tarps on the roof, three corners anchored by bricks, with the fourth blown up loose, flapping wildly in the wind. The three windows boarded up with mismatched planks of wood.

You drive faster, and what you see in front of you and the crunch of gravel under your tires makes your blood pump faster, makes you feel that cringe in your guts. You want to make some kind of an entrance but you know that's the whiskey talking. Nossir. No kind of time for an entrance. Be smart. Be normal.

You go through the front door almost unnoticed, and it depresses you until someone sticks a big glass of Jim Beam in your hand and you realize that someone is Sully. "Hey, big brother," he says, in that mocking way of his.

"Hey, fuckstick," you say back, swallowing and breathing deep.

"You're drunk, already. Good for you," Sully says. *Smug little piece of shit.* You look at him and remember tying his Cabbage Patch Kid to the ceiling fan when you were young, when the age difference meant something. You remember Sully howling in pity for the tortured doll, and you laughing.

"What's with the Cadillac?" you say.

"Nice, right? Wait till you see the rest of it. Come with me."

You follow your little brother through the front hall and into the library. Jerry Springer plays on his huge flat-screen TV, on mute, closed caption streaming across the bottom of the picture. A massive black woman holding a chair over her head is chasing a stick-thin white woman around the stage, calling her a whore and a home wrecker. The black woman charges like a gladiator finishing a kill. Her chest heaves. You read her words and think about how Jerry could get those chairs nailed to the floor to prevent this if he wanted. You stare at them all, at the screen, unable to turn away. The white woman kneels. The black woman picks up the chair again and raises it over her head like an ax above a log. Then two beefy guys restrain her and the fun ends. Sully is waiting, watching you watch. "Great, huh?" he says. You nod. Sully the choreographer.

The next room is full of people, a couple dozen of them, dressed up for the occasion. Overalls and wifebeaters and John Deere hats and all the boots. Everyone has shit-kicking boots on. Men have construction boots or cowboy boots, and most of the women do, too. You look at the women, starting with their feet, and your eyes stop on a pair of black stiletto-heeled boots. She's turned the other way, but you'd know her profile anywhere, the way those ass cheeks look in tight jeans, round and perfect like two halves of a melon. Katie Fee, the girl who got away, the girl too good for you and what you've become. Will you talk to her? You don't know. It's been almost ten years.

Your palms sweat.

You're on your own now, exposed. Sully has moved away from you, into the crowd. He high-fives a guy you don't recognize, a guy wearing a foam-mesh Nascar hat with Dale Earnhardt's face and a big #3 on it. Ugly as hell hat. Sully loves it. Everyone here turned out for Sully, for "Sully," like they always do. The heir apparent.

You're on your own now, with Katie Fee standing twenty feet away, wiggling her ass at you. Anne and the kids might or might not be coming. She screamed at you when you left, calling you a drunk and a bad father, after refusing to let you drive her and the kids to Sully's place. You started to argue, telling her that you could drive these back roads with your eyes shut and a whole bottle of whiskey in you. You knew you sounded like a perfect dickhead saying it, but you didn't care. Not today.

You need another drink. You throw back what's left of the

Beam and look for your next one. In the corner is a big metal basin, more of a tub, the kind used to bob for apples. Instead of apples it's full of iced-down Miller High Life. In cans, of course. You reach in deep and get one off the bottom, open it, and suck down half of it in three big swigs. Right. Okay. That's better. You breathe deep and relax a little. Maybe you will talk to Katie.

Just then Jake Montford walks up to you and starts jabbering in that fake way of his. He tells you about the latest toy he bought himself, a Ducati Multistrada. He wants to know when you're going to take your Harley out with him on the open road. That's what he says. He sees you looking at Katie Fee's ass, winking at you from just a few feet away. "You like that, huh?" Jake says. You look away, take another pull off your beer, pretend not to hear him. He wants to think you two have a bond, some kind of pact among the guilty, but you won't let him put you in his company. The sick fuck.

The first time you saw the pictures of his wife on the Internet, Bill Mason showed them to you. You said you didn't believe it and he whipped out his cell phone, fired it up, and Jake's wife's tits were staring you right in the face from that little four-inch screen, under that cheesy orange cartoon logo of the Website, the guy with the big bug eyes and binoculars next to the letters: VoyeurVillage.com. You saw all of her. The next picture showed her posing with a banana. You couldn't believe your eyes. Jake had a deviant side, sure. Hell, he got three hookers for his bachelor party and had two of them snort lines of cocaine off his dick before they blew him. He'd been to Thailand a couple of times "for business," though you couldn't see what kind of business his law firm would have in Thailand. And his favorite movie was

The Ice Storm, the one where all the bored suburban couples use car keys in a bowl to swap partners. But the thing with his wife went way beyond what you thought he'd do. Nobody knew the whole story. Nobody knew for sure if Jake did this on his own or with Kerry's permission. Nobody discussed it. How could they?

"God, I'd love to have just one night with her," Jake says. "One hour even." His mouth hangs open too much, and he leans forward, nose up, as if he might sniff the air in front of him like some hungry, panting dog. Katie has him in knots. As drunk as you are, you can tell Jakie Boy is drunker. Seeing him standing there gawking puts an idea in your head.

You think you might have some fun. You let yourself watch Katie for a few seconds. Her hair hangs in a tight ponytail, pulled back above her ears, so you can see the sharp angle of her jaw and the laugh lines when she smiles. She has a black lace blouse that creeps up whenever she leans forward, showing the small of her back. You can remember touching her there and running your hand up and down over it—slowly, so nobody would notice, right there in the middle of the hourglass—when you danced with her at reunion almost ten years ago. Human League. Don't You Want Me. You almost passed out from the rush it gave you. The delicious curve of it. How solid it felt, lean and tight. She hadn't changed a bit, through all her troubles. The husband with the ball cancer that turned out to be fatal, the subsequent miscarriage that stole what was left of her life.

"Jakie," you say. "Let's go get a shot of something."

Jake eyes you suspiciously, then looks at Katie. "No," he says. "Let's go talk to her."

You knew that was coming. You shake your head, but your

brain nods. You think about the first words you will say to her.

"C'mon. What's the harm? We'll just mingle with her a little."

"Fine. Whatever."

"Great," Jakie says. "But you're right about the shots. I need something harder than beer for this." He disappears in pursuit of alcohol.

While Jake is gone, you survey the room. Walt Hagan, who's running for county controller, standing with his pea-brained wife, sister of Sully's wife, Jill. Walt followed Sully back after college, like some lost puppy, and has fed himself ever since with the crumbs from Sully's table, including Jill's poor sister. You were amazed that he actually had a chance to win the election. Two Christmases ago, he brought the eighteen-year-old daughter of one of the partners in the little accounting firm where he worked to Sully's Christmas party. He got her all hammered up on tequila and high on acid, then took her upstairs and had his way. Someone said she'd already passed out before Walt started in on her. You see George Battaglia, the big fat ex-cop turned real estate agent who has just been indicted on racketeering charges. Everyone knew where his money came from, but nobody talked about it. He'd been indicted once before, and everyone thought he'd beat this charge, too.

And Bobby Beck, the builder who made this house for Sully. You remember the long boozy conversations he and Sully had about the project. Way back, when your opinion counted for something and you were invited to such meetings. Twelve bedrooms and four distinct architectural designs, each specific to a period of the local history. Georgian, Colonial, Victorian—and one more you can't remember. Bobby has good looks and a kind of aura about him, like he can do anything. He and Jill get on well, too well you think. You wonder if something has happened between them. Probably not. It'd be career suicide for Bobby to mess with the Great Sully's wife. You look around the room where you stand, the library, with twelve-foot-high tray ceilings lined with eighteen-inch crown molding, the wide-plank reclaimed-wood floor. You have to hand it to Bobby: he's an artist. The house still knocks you out. You remember the house-warming party, after hours, when Sully took you all up to the cigar balcony. He shut off all the electricity at the circuit breaker, the generator kicked in, and then Sully gave a long speech about leaving the safety on until he said go. Then he went inside and came back out and handed out loaded rifles to every one of us. Yours was a Browning A-Bolt, but the rest got Winchesters. You stood out there smoking for half an hour or so, not knowing what he had in mind. Then he flipped on the floodlight and trained it on the dark woods behind his house. The light bounced off what seemed like hundreds of nickels suspended in midair. Then you saw the deer feeder and realized what you were looking at. "Let 'em have it, boys," Sully said. The five of you on that deck must've killed fourteen deer, including three mature bucks, the largest of which was a twelve-pointer.

Antlers on the wall, above the fireplace. Your eyes drop and you notice Uncle Pete, the one who had the FBI crawling all over the whole family for years after threatening the building inspector publicly, at a hearing, just three months before the inspector ended up at the bottom of the Hudson. Uncle George, the one who did the deed, was dying by then, of liver cancer. So they did have some kind of plan. You see your mother, already more than half pissed, slurring her words as she speaks to David Mann, head of Hudson Gas. You see Sue Baker, who will give almost any guy with a hard-on and a hundred a quickie if there's a bathroom or a closet nearby. She calls it cab fare, like she's Audrey Hepburn running off to meet that A-Team guy at Tiffany's.

Fuck 'em all. You can tell the way they look at you or avoid looking at you. You can tell that they have loaded up all their Judge Guns and pointed them straight at your head and fired away until you're dead to them all. Well, so be it.

Speaking of judging, there's Judge Wilkins, the one your dad paid off to keep you out of jail after the second DWI. Wilkins stands about six feet two and has lean, chiseled features like he belongs in some sepia photo essay about the Great Depression. There he stands, at the Second Quinqennial Sullapalooza, sipping Scotch and looking all high and mighty. Thank God Wilkins caught your next case, too—the one that had you wandering in the woods and smoking the spliff with the retard. The Hand of Fate, Wilkins called it when you went to go see him about it. "Son, do you believe in God?" he asked you. You saw the cross around his neck and said you did, of course. "Well, He must have some kind of plan for you, because you really shouldn't be standing here. You should either be locked up or dead. The Hand of Fate intervened, though. Along with your good family. So you're getting yet another chance. Do something with it, son."

Bullshit, you remember thinking. Hand of Sully, not fate. Sully and your father arranged to pay off this crooked Atticus Finch wannabe motherfucker and guarantee him a win in the next election if he made the trouble go away. And that's what he did, in return for twenty thousand dollars, wrapped in a brown paper bag, just like in the movies. Later you started thinking about what Wilkins said: the Hand of Fate. You had to admit that Fate had played some kind of role in your life, on that night and before. Fate made you a member of the Sullivan clan, heir to the largest land-owning family in Dutchess County. Fate made you bad at school and only so-so at sports. Fate made you want more sex than you needed or was good for you. Fate gave you a taste for booze and drugs. Fate gave your little brother—the one you used to beat on and defend at school, the one you taught how to play soccer and football and French kiss and fuck—all the business genes in the whole family. Fate made it possible for Sully, whom everyone now called Sully after the original John Daniel "Sully" Sullivan, the one who built up this twisted fortune in the first place, to put the pieces back together after the loan defaults of the eighties and FBI investigation of the nineties. Sully, Sully Junior, the Boy Wonder, the Fixer, *El Jefe*, from whom everyone in the family now takes orders, gladly, so long as the family fleet of Range Rovers gets paid for and the monthly allowance keeps flowing. Fate gave the family Sully to save it from itself. Fate put you at your ten-year reunion with Katie Fee just after she was widowed. And Fate saved your ass, too, on the day you smashed your brand-new black Range Rover, your second one in two years, into the minivan full of kids out on Route 9.

Crazy how little of it you remember now, almost exactly five years later. You know that because it happened after the first Sullapalooza, and coming here today you had some vague notion that this would be your triumphant return to the scene, a way to show all these people that you might be down but not out. Not yet. But you should be, and you knew it. You left here in a hurry, running off to meet Tina, the little waitress at Charlie Brown's Steakhouse you'd been seeing on the side. You swerved your way over there fine, without incident, and you took her to the usual spot: Courtyard Inn by Marriott. Not a rent-by-the-hour place, sure, but not the Ritz, either. But to Tina, it was the ultimate luxury. And it made you happy that it gave her such a thrill. So you went there and put down a whole bottle of red wine and got your own kind of thrill with her, and within minutes you were dressed and back behind the wheel of the Range Rover, heading toward Route 9. You stopped at the 7-Eleven on the corner of Old Post and Route 9.

You can actually remember seeing the cop car in the parking lot and thinking to yourself how very fucked up it would be if you drunk-drove right into that cop car. What you didn't know then is that the car belonged to the guy standing beside you at the coffee machine, the fat guy in the jean jacket, a just-off-duty cop who had kept an eye on you while he was paying for his fat cop meal at the cash register. Thank God he also worked part-time as a security guard at one of your family's self-storage locations, the creatively named Sully's Storage in Hopewell. That's how Sully got to him and convinced him he didn't ever get a good look at you.

You started shoving that muffin down your craw with one hand and started up the Range Rover and cranked up Dexys Midnight Runners on the stereo with the other hand, but both your eyes fixed on that cop and his holstered gun and stayed on him until you felt the sickening crunch of metal as you smashed into the minivan. In the muffled cockpit of your Range Rover, the impact was more felt than heard, but you rolled down your window in time to hear the sound of the bumper come loose and hit the blacktop to the soundtrack of "Come On, Eileen." You whirled around and saw the terror on the woman's face. You heard her scream. You put the Rover into drive and started to pull away, but hesitated. You saw Fat Cop break into a run toward the cop car. You must've telegraphed your intentions somehow. Some vigilante dude ran over and stuck his hand in your open window to try to grab the keys, but you pulled it deeper than he wanted it to go and smashed him in the face with your open hand. Enough to be rid of him. And you were off.

Ten minutes later you led Fat Cop on the first high-speed police chase in twenty years in Dutchess County. You remember the moment you decided to go for it, thinking irrationally about Fat Cop's size and how you used to run cross country and how you knew the trails from when the family owned horses. Your Range Rover was black and built for off-road driving. You remember thinking you had no choice: one more DWI would take your license forever and put you in jail for a long, long time. The adrenaline kicked in, made you feel piss-drunk and doomed and invincible. You heard the squeal of your tires and their impact on the curb as you jumped it, and figured Fat Cop wouldn't follow and you'd gain a few seconds. You were right.

Everything is a blur after that, but you could piece it together later on, and memories surfaced over time and became indistinguishable from what you read and what people told you had happened. The chase covered five miles on Route 9, and the police report said it took under three minutes. You found the turn you wanted, the one that led you to the ass-end of Netherwood Road. You knew that stretch of the road. You knew a trail not far away that led deep into the woods. Don't crash, you told yourself. Focus. And then you turned onto Netherwood and shut your lights off and hit the four-wheel-drive button and minutes later you drove through an opening in the woods, hoping that the chrome on your bumper didn't catch any passing headlights. At one point your right two tires went flat, but that was about the time you realized that you didn't hear the siren anymore. You listened to your own breathing, trying to think and stay calm. You stopped the truck and got out and you ran. And ran. You stayed in those woods all night, then you called Sully as soon as the sun came up. He picked you up and took you to the bus station. You ran your mouth at him the whole time, but he said nothing but this, "Here's two thousand in cash. It's all I have. Get on a bus and go someplace far away. Don't call me. Not this week. Give me at least a week to figure things out." You eventually caught a bus to one place, then another, then out to the North Fork of Long Island, where Anne has relatives. That's where you were when you found out why the cop siren stopped. A parking garage collapsed at the Poughkeepsie Galleria mall, and all police within fifty miles got called to the scene. So soon after 9/11, they assumed it was a terrorist attack, so they all went running over there for their piece of glory. Ha. The Hand of Fate. And here you are, five years almost to the day, back at the scene where that night began. No more family-issue Range Rover, but you still have your freedom; and, after a nine-month suspension, your driver's license is yours to lose again.

Somebody tugs your shirt. "Hey, wake up. I know you said you didn't want one, but this is the good stuff. Johnny Walker Blue. Compliments of Sully." Jake Montford has returned, ready for action. He nods in the direction of Katie. You take the drink from him, ditch your beer can on a nearby table, and take a big sip of whiskey. "Okay," you say. "Let's do this before I change my mind."

But Katie has moved away from you. She's in the next room, the living room, next to a roasted pig suspended on a spit over the biggest Sterno flame you've ever seen. She's talking to another woman you don't recognize. You and Jake move toward them. Before you reach them, Sully's wife, Jill, and their son, Sully Junior, stop you to say hello. Jill hugs you and so does little Sully and you remember the invitation said this was doubling as a birthday party for the tyke, who turned three last week. You have no gift.

"Look what your idiot brother gave little Sully for his birthday," Jill says. You look down at his little moon face and you breathe slowly, trying not to seem as drunk as you are. "His shirt," Jill says. The shirt says HUNG LIKE A 10-YEAR-OLD in big black letters. You laugh out loud.

Jill moves away, probably happy to escape Jake Montford, whose little photography fetish has become an open secret. On the other side of the buffet setup in the living room are the big floor-to-ceiling windows overlooking the pond. You can see the fading sunlight bouncing off the water and a bunch of kids, with nannies in tow, feeding a flock of mallards at the water's edge. As Jill and Sully Jr. walk away, you remember the wording on the invitation: "The Quinquennial Sullapalooza: A Redneck Revival—plus birthday bash for SullyBoy! 2pm 'til whenever. Kid-friendly 'til dark. Redneck attire only. Dress like you mean it." You pull out your phone and see it blinking back—four text messages from Anne. You put it back in your pocket.

It's almost dark, and you're in no shape to talk to Katie Fee. Words won't come easy, especially after you finish this next whiskey. You think about breaking off but decide against it, afraid to leave her alone with Jake.

When you reach them, Katie and her friend are talking about the party, marveling over Sully's stagecraft. Apparently there are hayrides and a huge Moon Bounce for the kids out back, and the Wine Barn has been turned into a Moonshine Barn, complete with a functioning still and authentic poteen shipped in from Ireland. Introductions are made, and Katie smiles at you and kisses your cheek. A cloud of her smell hits you like a drug. Grit and glam—less like perfume and more like soap and sweat. You feel suddenly bolder. You decide to ignore the trace of pity—or regret?—you see in her eyes. Given what she's been through, it probably has nothing to do with you.

"Ladies, meet Jake Montford."

Jake bows like he's some kind of nobleman meeting debutantes. You throw back the rest of the Johnny Walker Blue in a single gulp. Katie's friend looks you and Jake up and down and excuses herself to go find her boyfriend.

"It's good to see you, Katie," you say, hoping you can control where this goes.

"You, too," she says, and she seems sincere. You want Jake gone. You want to tell Katie everything you didn't say that night at reunion. You know it's the idea of her more than it is *her*. It's her looks and the way she talks softly, and the fact that she still seems innocent after all the living she's done.

Jake breaks the silence. "Katie, if my wife weren't standing across the room, I'd make a move on you. How is it that you've stayed single? Don't any of these guys have any balls?" He's looking at her hand. He doesn't know about her dead husband.

You hear your name being called. You turn around and see

Anne coming toward you. Your children, Andrew and Lily, Irish twins at six and five, are on either side of her, each holding one of her hands. "There you are," she says. You are at once glad to see them and deeply depressed. You force a smile and gather up both kids in a big hug. "You smell like medicine," Lily says. Anne says hello to Katie and Jake.

"Come on," you say. "Let's go for a hayride while we still can."

You say quick goodbyes to Katie and Jake and lead your family out the back door, past the pig on a spit still getting its ass roasted by that giant Sterno and the catered buffet and the tubs of beer and bar tended by an overalls-wearing employee of the catering company. You enter the backyard through huge French doors and you step out onto a slate patio. The patio fire pit is already going, stacked high with burning logs cut from the surrounding woods. You see the hayride in the distance behind the pond, a giant wagon towed by a John Deere, making a broad, slow circle. Then you see a bunch of the older kids playing what looks like some kind of a football or rugby game. They're all chasing in a circle inside a makeshift pen made out of garden fencing. Then you realize—they're chasing a greased pig. Lily and Andrew love it and they beg you to let them join the chase. You tell them to ask their mother. Anne says yes, and the kids go running.

Now you're alone with your wife. Neither of you speak for a minute but just watch your kids run off to chase the pig. "It's great fun," Anne says. "I've got to give your brother credit. He knows how to throw a party."

You nod.

A minute later, Anne says, "So how drunk are you?"

You don't answer.

"Are you coming home tonight?"

You stay quiet.

"Well, please be careful. I'm going to say goodbye to your family and take the kids home as soon as this pig thing is over. They're going to be covered in mud, and I'm not in the mood to hang out with a bunch of drunk parents who've offloaded their kids to the help."

"I hear you," you say. And you really do hear her. She's right and you know it.

"I'll be okay. I'll stay here tonight and I'll see you guys first thing in the morning."

"Sure you will," Anne says, and she walks away from you toward the pigpen without looking back.

You stand there watching her and your children move away from you, and you think of Katie. You think about how you have everything Katie has lost. You let them go.

You find the nearest beer tub and fish one out. This time it's a Pabst Blue Ribbon. You turn and head back inside, looking for Katie.

When you reach them, Jake has his arm behind Katie, not quite touching her, and is explaining how Sully pulled off the stunt with the Cadillac in the front yard. They can't see you. The sacrificial pig is still bathing in Sterno flames beside them. You pause and listen. "Right," Jake says. "It's amazing. So the guys down at Wayne's Salvage owed him one, and he got them to come flip the Caddy over and put a little motor on the axel so the front wheels keep spinning. The fire was just a burn barrel full of fire wood. He put it behind the engine hood so you can't see it when you're coming up the driveway...."

"Brilliant," Katie says, just before they both notice you. Then she excuses herself to go to the bathroom.

"You're coming back, right?" Jake says, touching her hand. You could kill him right here and now.

Katie smiles and nods and lets her hand rest on his for an extra beat.

Jake turns to you. "God*damn*, she's hot," he says, but you can hardly hear him. You lift your beer and pour half of it down your throat while Jakie Boy keeps talking. "Thanks, man. I think you're right. I think she really might be into it."

"Into what?" you say.

"You know. I think she might be into hanging out later with me and Kerry."

You ball up your fists, trying to focus and think about what to do. Your lips burn. You want to kill him with your bare hands. You wonder what kind of time you'd do if you strangle him right here. With your history, you could definitely plead insanity. Do the math. You can hear yourself breathing. You say nothing.

Jake takes half a step away from you and looks at you funny. Scared. "What's up, man?"

He's looking at your hand, which is balled up and cocked back, waiting for you to decide what to do with it. You realize what you're going to do, and you try to make your face calm. You smile. You breathe. You think about angles and distance and how you need to make it count. Then you shake your head a little and say, "You know what this is, Jakie?"

"What? What do you mean?" he says, taking another step backward.

"This is the hand of fate." You swing as hard as you can, a home-run swing, but you pop it foul, barely clipping the bottom of his chin. He's stunned. You rush him. You try to recover some control. "It's okay. I didn't mean it," you say over and over again. "We're okay." You hug Jake Montford, your hands on either side of his head, then his shoulders, then his head—like you're two worn-out boxers in the ninth round. "It's okay. I'm a little drunk."

You're standing there, now just a couple of feet from the pig on a spit, and you can see its pig eyes looking up and the flame still hitting its blackened skin as the spit turns. You're out of breath. Your hands still rest on Jake Montford's head, and you bring them forward, down his neck, then up again to his cheeks. You stare into his eyes, then the pig eyes, and back to Jake. You can feel sweat on the back of his neck and his pulse going wild. "It's okay, Jakie. I'm a little drunk is all."

Jake starts laughing, but it's more of a cough, meant to defuse the situation. He's terrified. He knows what you've done, what you're capable of. Time is short. You say, "Hang on. Wait a minute. I want to talk to you about something. It's important. Seriously."

"What?" he says.

"No big deal," you say, still trying to figure all this out. "It's no big deal. It's just... just that..." You hang your head, as if gathering your thoughts. As if you might cry. You breathe deep. It's time.

"What, man? What? Are you okay?"

"It's just that if you ever so much as look at Katie Fee again, I will kill you." Then you grab his ears tight enough so that there's no way he can break loose, and you pull your head back, bend your knees, and launch yourself at him. You snap your neck forward at the same time and ram the top of your forehead as hard as you can into his nose. You feel the impact, solid like a hammer against a walnut. You feel it crunch, and it makes you happy. You laugh. Then you push Jake Montford headfirst into the flaming pig on a spit and you begin moving toward the French doors, where the last hayride is just returning. You wonder if you're too late to go home with Anne and your kids, and you think about how long it would take you on foot.

You decide to walk faster.

POOR JIMMY

"It's gonna get weird," Jimmy said. "It's about to get really weird."

I looked at him but said nothing.

"Check out the gazelles," he said, pointing with his chin.

Three women had gathered at the far end of the bar. Jimmy calls unescorted women in bars "gazelles." If they're drunk or otherwise vulnerable, then they're "wounded gazelles," like the ones that get taken down by hungry lions on National Geographic. These women at the end of the bar weren't drunk and looked anything but vulnerable. Safe bet they were models or actresses, given where we were, an unmarked members-only club in downtown Manhattan that caters to the professionally beautiful. The women fit the room, which had twenty-foot ceilings, huge windows overlooking the Meatpacking District from a high floor, long leather couches, and a massive stainless-steel bar. The women, two brunettes and a blonde, were almost young enough to be Jimmy's daughters and were drawing Cro-Magnon stares from all the slobs in the place, us included. They seemed inured to it.

Jimmy had the perfect setup. The L-shaped bar hadn't filled up yet. The women stood at the corner of the L, as if on a small stage, while we sat on stools halfway down its long stretch. Jimmy already had a beer and two tequila shots in him, even though we'd only been there an hour or so. When he wants to drink, he doesn't mess around. Says he doesn't like to do anything "half-assed." By now I knew that I'd gotten Fun Jimmy tonight, not one of the other Jimmys, and it gave me hope that my plan might actually succeed.

"Be right back," Jimmy said, dismounting his stool. He grabbed his drink and sashayed toward the three women. Just before he reached them, he turned to me and grinned like an idiot. He licked two fingers, turned and reached them out toward the blonde's head, moving them to within inches, then withdrew them quickly as if he'd touched a flame. A guy behind me laughed out loud. Then Jimmy tapped the blonde on the shoulder and started talking, and I could see them clench up and look at each other. Jimmy always says that it's tough to be a really pretty girl: you're screwed no matter what. You don't want to be catcalled and bothered by the males of the species, but you want to dress up and feel pretty, like any girl. If you go through all the trouble of making yourself look as good as you can look and no guy pays attention to you, you'll be upset about it. So you want the attention, but then you get annoyed when you get it. Screwed no matter what.

Sure enough, the women looked like they hated Jimmy's guts when he first approached them. But minutes later, whatever nonsense came spilling out of his mouth started putting them at ease. One of them laughed, then cupped her hand over her mouth and ran it down her chin, as if trying to wipe away her amusement. The other two also loosened up. Jimmy kept going and quickly had them all giggling and shaking their heads.

After a few minutes of this, Jimmy signaled me to come over. I moved over a couple of stools and joined the edge of the group.

"Murph, let me introduce you to Katie, Allison, and Rayna, the three best-looking girls in New York City. We were just talking about how embarrassing it is to buy condoms. You know. Because the checkout girl knows exactly what you're going to do with them. And she's actually got to touch the box so she can scan it.

The whole thing is weird. Plus, what if she needs to call over the store intercom for a price check? Anyway, ladies, let me introduce you to Will Murphy, my gay Army buddy. Murph here was by far the bravest homosexual in our battalion. He also happens to be an avid consumer of condoms."

The women didn't know what to do with that—so they just laughed. One of them asked about my wedding ring, and Jimmy said, "Don't ask, don't tell, but he's from Massachusetts where that sort of stuff is legal. Good thing, too. The ring is what kept him from getting his ass kicked in Iraq."

I thought about going along with it, but instead I said, "Don't listen to my homophobic, misogynist friend here. The Army part is true. But the rest of it is bullshit. I'm not gay, I'm not very brave, and I am married—to a woman."

"How long?" the blonde, Allison, asked.

"Ten years this December."

"Wow, that's great," she said. "Any kids?"

"Two boys—four and two."

"Yep. And he's not done yet," Jimmy said, sticking an elbow in my ribs.

Allison looked at me, her eyebrows raised. "My wife Jenny and I are expecting our third—a girl."

They all said congratulations, and Jimmy raised his glass to toast my unborn daughter. His eyes flickered back and forth, a sign of his mind changing channels, looking for better entertainment. He took a huge swig from his third tequila, put the glass on the bar, and said, "Speaking of kids, I need to drop a couple off at the pool. Excuse me, ladies. I really need to make Number Two, and Murph tells me this place has a bathroom so clean you can eat off the toilet seats."

"Jesus, Jimmy," I said. "Did we really need to know that?" But I was talking to the back of his head as he was walking toward the bathroom. The girls shook their heads in disgust, but I got the sense that they enjoyed the crudeness.

I ordered myself another beer and told the bartender to bring another round for our new friends. The bar had filled up around us, and I noticed that we'd attracted an audience. Not we—them. The women. People lined the bar now on both sides of us, and all the men were looking, or obviously trying not to look, at Katie, Allison, and Rayna—probably wondering why the hell they were letting me stand so close to them.

Myself, I found it difficult to make eye contact with them. So I tried making more small talk while staring at my beer. I asked them what they did. Rayna and Katie were fashion models, here for some kind of reality-TV show. Allison had an online show about the stock market and called herself a video blogger. At one point, Rayna, who had seemed completely bored up to this point, asked me if I was over in Iraq like Jimmy. I nodded, and she perked up.

"Do you mind talking about it? What was it like?"

"For me, it was boring. A lot of waiting, a lot of paperwork, and miscommunication with the Iraqis. I sort of had a desk job within the Green Zone. Jimmy had a different experience."

"So you didn't see combat and he did?"

"Something like that."

"What's the worst thing that happened to you over there?"

The question surprised me. People hardly ever asked me about Iraq, and when they did, they focused on the banal stuff, the food, the weather, the anti-Americanism, and so on. I faced Rayna and for the first time met her eyes, which were green and full of intelligence. She had pale white skin and a long neck that the camera must've loved. Her nose was longer than it seemed from a distance, and crooked—pointed slightly to one side. It made her even better looking. It made me wish my wife were skinny again. It made me wish that I weren't married and Rayna were a wounded gazelle. It made me want to tell her the truth.

"A suicide bomber got into the Zone one time right after the first election," I said. "She was an older woman who'd been coming in for a while to babysit some of our translators' kids. She was familiar to us all. We had come to trust her. She blew herself up less than ten feet from me, and a first sergeant standing next to me took the brunt of the explosion. Will Keane. Blew off his leg above the knee and severed his femoral artery. We couldn't help him."

I'd never stopped looking at Rayna while telling this story. I realized I hadn't told the full story to anyone else—not even Jenny. Not even Jimmy. Wasn't supposed to. The incident became classified and had never been reported in the news because the brass didn't want it to get out that Americans were dying within the Green Zone. I'd tried to push the whole thing out of my head.

Right now I looked at Rayna and she looked back at me, unblinking, her jaw set in a way that pulled back the corners of her mouth into a small smile. "I'm sorry," she said with an even tone. "Were you close to him?" I nodded and looked at the other two women, who were both shaking their heads and looking down at the bar. "He was only twenty-eight. He told me I'd be godfather to his first kid if he ever had one. Jimmy knew him, too."

Speaking of, where the hell was he? He'd been gone forever.

The one named Katie reached out and put her hand on my shoulder. "That must've been horrible," she said. "It must still be horrible. I can't… I can't even imagine."

Rayna started to ask me another question, but Jimmy came back and stepped between us, his arm outstretched. He looked at the women, then at me.

"Way to go, Murph. I see you're keeping them laughing, as always. He's a barrel of fun, isn't he, girls? Watch yourselves, now. Make way for me, folks. My mission isn't over."

The three women made way for Jimmy, their eyes pinned on him. His face was flushed, and his hair damp, as if from sweat. At first, I couldn't tell what he held in his hand. He held it above his head and called for the bartender to come over. What was he up to now?

A hush rippled over the bar, as it came into focus for everyone: Jimmy held an empty spool from a toilet-paper roll. He waved it at the bartender, telling him the bathroom had run out at the worst possible time. When the bartender reached him, Jimmy leaned forward and said in a mock whisper that was loud enough for the entire barroom to hear, "Sorry, man. This is really embarrassing. But I ran out of this and, well… you know. I need some more. It's kind of important. I've got a five-flusher on my hands in there."

The women, unable to stop laughing but clearly grossed out, started moving away from Jimmy, and everyone at the bar started cracking up. Jimmy pretended not to see any of it and just kept his eyes on the bartender, who was also laughing. It wasn't just Jimmy's very public request for more toilet paper at this velvet-rope club or his red face and sweaty brow or his poop talk in front of three stunningly beautiful women that the rest of the bar assumed he was trying to impress. The real punch line was that Jimmy had come back dragging a strip of toilet paper, about eight feet long, behind him, one end of it stuck to the bottom of his shoe, in plain sight of everyone sitting at the now-full bar. Nobody knew if the whole scene was real or staged, but everyone loved it.

That's pretty much the way it goes. Nobody knows quite what to make of him, but everyone loves Jimmy Dolan. The permanent twinkle in his eye, the barely contained mania, the buzzing life force that even two wars—including more than his fair share of heavy combat—couldn't kill. Ever since I met him in Desert Storm, or Desert Drizzle, as he derided it, he's been that kind of guy. The kind of guy who walks into a room and right away has every guy wanting to be his best friend and every woman wanting to get naked with him—that is, when he's not talking about five-flushers.

But Jimmy had been going through some rough times. He'd made a mess of things the last time he'd come to town, and my plan tonight was to try to clean it up for him. Almost twenty years ago, in the first Gulf War, half a dozen of us grunts from the 82nd Airborne who'd met in Fort Bragg had been shipped out as part of the same brigade and become inseparable. We did everything together—we fought (or at least pointed our rifles occasionally), we drank, we bucked authority, and we bitched nonstop about being glorified prison guards in a war that never was. Jimmy led us in our malaise and often shook us out of it, creating adventures out of whole cloth in the way that only he could. Like the time he got a mad crush on the Kuwaiti translator and went AWOL for a week so he could cross over and meet her family. I chased him down and dragged him back, and it's one of the dumbest things I've ever done. And one of the most fun.

Or the time one of our Kurdish helpers rode his scooter into our camp and got chased by the pregnant dog. Jimmy has a thing for animals, especially dogs, and he'd heard about this guy kicking this pregnant black Lab who'd become something of a mascot to us. On one particular day, Jimmy and the rest of us were standing around running our mouths, and the bitch came around as usual to beg for scraps from our MREs. In comes that Kurd on his scooter, and sure enough, that bitch took off after him, yapping her poor, stupid head off. The Kurd slowed down his bike to let her come near to him. Then when she was a few feet away, he stuck out his leg, throttled the bike, and landed his bootheel so hard in the dog's rib cage that she crashed to the ground, yelping and whimpering like she was dying. The Kurd knew we were watching and probably meant to fuck with us. He also knew he'd gone too far, and I could see the fear in his eyes when he turned around to see what we'd do. By then Jimmy had already taken off after him in a full sprint, running faster than I'd ever seen him run. The Kurd pushed off, gunned his engine, and tried to get away. But he was too late. Jimmy lunged at him and dive-tackled him off his scooter. The Kurd had some size on him but was no match for Jimmy. He didn't even try to fight back—was too scared. He started apologizing and screaming like a girl, but Jimmy didn't hear any of it and none of us tried to stop it for almost a full minute. He straddled the Kurd, pinning his arms back with his knees so he couldn't get off his back and he couldn't fight back. Then he ripped his helmet off and beat his face with both hands, like working on a speed bag, until he knocked him out. He was still swinging when we pulled him off. Put the Kurd in the hospital for a week. Guy had to have his jaw wired shut and lost two of his front teeth. We all covered for Jimmy, and he didn't get in any trouble.

The Kurd got a big dose of Rescue Jimmy, one of the Jimmys who came out a little too often and usually got us into trouble. But we loved him for it. We all wanted to do the same thing to that Kurd for kicking our bitch, but Jimmy is the guy who actually *did* it.

After the war we all stayed in touch and got together at least a couple of times a year. Everyone except Jimmy got married and had kids, and all of us except one went back over to help finish the job after 9/11. That's when Jimmy and J.O.B. and Stevie went north and saw the real deal up in Fallujah, while I was busy designing airfields in Qatar.

That's also when Jimmy started to kind of lose it, I guess. Life had started catching up with him, and he knew it. We got shipped out to different places and rarely saw each other over there, but I'd get email updates from "Harlem"—which was Jimmy's code name for Fallujah, since he couldn't say where he was. During one of the few times we got to see each other while deployed, he admitted to me that reenlisting after 9/11 felt like the meatheaded move of the century to him. He didn't like the war, didn't like the mission, didn't want to kill anymore. He'd just had some incident at a checkpoint where one of the guys in his platoon took out a couple of civilians. It hit him hard. This was after it became clear that the whole war was kind of a sham, and it seemed unwinnable to us on the ground. The hopelessness started eating Jimmy from the inside.

They say you marry the person you're with when you're ready to get married, and that's what sort of happened with the rest of us. We all had girlfriends before Desert Storm, a few of whom got passed back and forth. Army skanks from Fort Bragg. Three of the guys married their girlfriends between deployments overseas, just so they'd have someone to go home to. I knew Jenny from school and didn't start dating her until after Desert Storm. But we got engaged after only four months, and were married and pregnant within a year. I always thought I wanted a big family. Work went well for me so I thought I could afford it. I'd started a corporate security business after Desert Storm and hired a bunch of guys from the 82nd. After 9/11, I kept the business going while deployed overseas and it really took off. I never thought I'd make that much money.

In terms of settling down, Jimmy was the odd man out. He never married and only recently had a serious girlfriend—a forty-five-year-old woman with two teenage sons. At one point he told me he loved her and wanted to marry her, but things went sideways with them. It ended badly, and Jimmy felt terrible about abandoning the two boys. The breakup hit him hard and he started drinking heavily.

All this was blowing up on Jimmy the last time we all got together in New York. The night ended when Jimmy got offended and flew into a rage just like he did with the Kurd. The night had gone along fine, with the usual amount of drinking and the obligatory trip to the strip club that got us all hot and bothered and talking about kids and wives and monogamy and not getting what we bargained for and all that male bullshit that goes along with nights like that. Anyhow, we drank too much and comments were made, and things turned ugly. At the end of it Jimmy got fired up and ended up cracking J.O.B. pretty good in the face. He and Jimmy hadn't spoken since, but tonight was the night they were supposed to hug it out. Only Jimmy didn't know that yet, and neither did J.O.B. I planned to get Jimmy drunk to wear down his defenses, take him back to that same strip club we went to with the boys, and tell him there, where we could put the whole event into its proper context before J.O.B. showed up. If Jimmy behaved, I figured, J.O.B. would follow his lead.

I was doing all this at the urging of my wife, Jenny, who feels sorry for Jimmy Dolan and worries about him a lot. She said I had an obligation to help smooth things over because J.O.B. worked for me. I could bring everyone together and patch things up. Thing is, Jenny didn't know why Jimmy hit J.O.B., and I couldn't tell her.

"Poor Jimmy," she always says, no matter what version of Jimmy is showing himself. I used to argue with her about it, telling her that Jimmy had a great life, had everything going for him and didn't need her pity. Jimmy used to call her for advice on relationships and so on. I wondered what was said in those phone calls. Whatever it was, I think it made Jenny worry more for him. She didn't buy his clown act. She told me it was just a matter of time until he melted down completely. To her, he's always been Poor Jimmy.

Right after paying the cover charge at Scores, the strip club, Jimmy pointed toward a guy in a suit standing guard over the floor. "I think I know that guy," he said. "Holy shit. It's definitely gonna get weird." Within ten minutes, Jimmy had a new best friend in the manager on duty—Paul, I think his name was. It turns out that Paul had come back from Iraq eight months ago, and they knew a lot of people in common.

Within half an hour, Jimmy had his shirt off and was pole-dancing on a side stage to a dance remix of "Like a Virgin." At first it scared the real dancers and annoyed the customers, but Jimmy was actually pretty good at it, and the crowd began cheering him on and drinking more—so Paul let him finish the entire song.

When Jimmy finished his dance, I had a beer and a shot of Jameson waiting for him at a table away from the stage and stripper poles.

"So you remember last time were came here, right?"

"Sure. It's the last night I spoke to J.O.B."

"Right, well. J.O.B. is going to meet us tonight at midnight. We're supposed to tell him where to go. He wants to talk things out," I lied.

"That makes one of us."

"You're really willing to throw away a twenty-year friendship over some stupid drunken comments?"

"I have enough friends. So do you, Murph."

"Look, Jimmy. I know. I'm the one who should be pissed. I'm the one who should have hit him, and I'm okay with the whole thing. J.O.B. has always been sort of a shithead, but he's our shithead. I don't think he meant anything by it."

Jimmy just stared straight ahead for a moment. Then he took down his shot of Jameson in a single gulp.

"Well, are you willing to meet him?"

"Why are you ambushing me with this now?"

"Because I didn't think you'd come otherwise."

"You were right about that. Do you know what he said about Jenny?"

"Yes, Jimmy. I know." But something in Jimmy's face made me think that maybe I didn't know all of it.

Here's what I did know: That night, with J.O.B. and the rest of the guys from the 82nd, after watching the strippers at Scores for a couple of hours, we moved on to Molly Malone's, an Irish pub on Third Avenue. Everyone started talking about which stripper he liked best, and talk eventually turned to marriage and whether or not it was natural for a man to be with the same woman for the rest of his life.

At one point, I got up to go to the bathroom and, when I got back, J.O.B. cut right to the chase. "I can say for myself that it's been eight years with Angie, but it feels like eighty. She's nothing like she was before we got married, before the kids came. I definitely didn't sign up to have my balls cut off and be nagged into an early grave."

The line of conversation made me uncomfortable. J.O.B. worked for me, and Jenny and I really liked Angie. "You always get more than you bargain for with marriage," I said, trying to find a trapdoor.

"Yeah, Murph. You got about three times what you bargained for," J.O.B. said.

Jimmy sat straight up in his seat and pointed a finger at J.O.B. Jimmy has always loved my wife. "What did you say, O'Brien?"

"I said that Murph here got about three times what he bargained for. Jenny has put on some weight is all I'm saying."

"You need to take that back, O'Brien."

"Come on, Jimmy. You have to admit it's true. She does shake the floor when she walks into the room."

In a single motion, Jimmy launched himself at J.O.B. and his balled-up fist connected solidly with J.O.B.'s cheekbone with a sickening *thwack*.

That was my memory, but sitting here, looking at Jimmy, I knew there was more to it. Suddenly I didn't want to meet up with J.O.B. anymore. I didn't want to know what else J.O.B. did to piss off Jimmy. I wanted another drink and another one after that. And maybe a dance from one of the strippers. I wanted the night to keep pinwheeling out of control like the best nights with Jimmy often do.

"We don't need to meet up with him," I said.

Jimmy's eyes widened. "Really? Well, let's take a break from thinking about it and focus on our drinking. We're not supposed to meet him until midnight, anyhow, right? We've got time."

We ordered another round and then another. A Russian stripper came over and grabbed Jimmy by the arm and offered him a free dance. Two for one, she said. He walked away with her and I just sat there, drinking more. At some point I got some dances, too, but the memory of it is hazy. I can remember long legs and thong underwear and tits in my face and the feeling of being turned on and repulsed all at once. I remember wanting to get out of there and go home to Jenny. I started drinking water to sober up.

At some point I'd had enough and went looking for Jimmy. He sat at a side table next to a stage where his Russian was dancing on a pole. Her eye makeup had run on one side of her face. She looked like she'd been crying. Jimmy was talking on a cell phone that wasn't his. Yelling, more like it. He was saying something about immigration and deportation and it sounded like he was making threats.

"Jimmy, what're you doing?"

"Talking to Katya's fucknut boyfriend," he said. He didn't sound coherent. "She had a bruise on her shoulder. I asked her what it was. Says he threw her down the steps."

I grabbed the phone and hung up on Fucknut. Then I grabbed Jimmy's arm and stood him up. "Let's get out of this place," I said. "Let's get something to eat."

A few minutes later we walked out of there and I steered Jimmy past a crowded bar with a bunch of cops out front, keeping an eye on things. Just past the bar, we found a Dunkin' Donuts that advertised a flatbread egg sandwich, served twenty-four hours. Breakfast anytime, it said.

"It's about to get weird," Jimmy said under his breath as we came through the door. "It's about to get really weird."

He sounded unsteady, his words slow and deliberate and a little slurred. The walking around must've triggered the full effects of the last few drinks he slammed down.

The guy behind the counter had dark skin and spoke with an accent that might've been Iraqi. Perfect cherry on top of the night, I thought. We ordered sandwiches and water and sat in a booth in silence for what seemed like twenty minutes.

It was then that Jimmy told me what J.O.B. had said: "He called Jenny a pig. He said, 'Now that Murph has some money, why doesn't he dump that pig and trade her in for a little hottie?'"

"Thanks, asshole. Thanks for telling me that. Now I probably need to fire him, and he's one of my best sales guys."

Jimmy took a deep breath, stood up, and approached the counter. "Hey, chiefy, where are the sandwiches?"

"Coming, boss. Coming."

"We're pretty damn hungry over here."

"Coming, boss."

"Okay, but it's gonna get really weird in here in a second. In fact, if those sandwiches don't hit our table by the time I count to ten, it's going to get really weird in here really fast."

"Okay. Whatever you say, boss."

Jimmy started counting to ten before I could say anything. The guy behind the counter ignored him. When he hit ten, Jimmy opened the drink refrigerator, reached one arm inside, and started clearing out the plastic bottles. They went flying everywhere.

Jimmy backed up to look at what he'd done, and he bumped into the poster stand advertising the flatbread sandwich. He stopped and looked at it, and then he screamed, "Where are you?" Then he shoved it. It rocked back and forth and smacked him in the head. Then he punched the sign and knocked it down. He made a terrible clatter, and the guy behind the counter started going crazy and yelling, "Police! Police!" Then he disappeared out the front door to get the police.

I reached down and shook Jimmy and told him what was happening. We both scrambled to put the place back together. We put all the drinks back in the refrigerator and stood the sign back up, just as two cops, one black and one white, came through the front door, led by the counter guy, "That's him," he said, pointing at Jimmy.

Jimmy turned around as if looking for the culprit.

"Hey, officers. What's the problem?" Jimmy said, sounding

perfectly sober.

They just shrugged and shook their heads.

"Jesus, look at the time," Jimmy said. "Have a great night, fellas."

As we walked past the counter guy, Jimmy grabbed his arm, leaned over and whispered, "Now *that* was weird, wasn't it?"

"That was an asshole thing to do, wasn't it?" Jimmy said when we got back out onto the street.

I nodded. The brush with consequence had sobered Jimmy up, but he wasn't willing to let the night end here.

"Well, I've got to redeem myself, and I know just the way to do it." He pulled his cell phone out and started fiddling with it.

"Let's call it a night, man. I don't want to meet J.O.B. Let's quit while we're ahead."

"Nope. Call him and tell him we've had a change of plans. Tell him to meet you at Jimmy's Corner on West 44th. You're right. We should meet up with him."

Reluctantly, I did just that, but I did get Jimmy to agree to walk all the way there, so he'd keep sobering up before J.O.B. got there.

Jimmy's Corner has a long narrow bar with a few stools at one end, near the entrance. We grabbed those stools and bar-owner Jimmy, a retired boxer, came right over to us with two shots of Jameson and two pints of Guinness. He and my Jimmy had become friendly over the years, bonding over their shared name and shared passion for boxing. I had some hope again that the night could be saved.

We had two more rounds of shots and beers before J.O.B. arrived. He had no idea that Jimmy would be there, and I saw a look of genuine fear when he walked up to us and saw Jimmy for the first time since he'd hit him.

"Oh shit," he said before regaining his composure. I could tell that he'd been drinking, too. "I surrender," he said to Jimmy with a smile. "Just don't beat my ass again."

"It's all good," said Jimmy, and the two shook hands. Jimmy ordered another round of shots and beers for all of us and then announced that he had to take a piss.

He was gone for a long time, so long that I wondered if he was going to repeat his performance from the start of the night. I took the opportunity to calm J.O.B. down and get him to agree to make peace.

We spent a few minutes reliving the old days before they showed up. Allison and Rayna could not have been more out of place at Jimmy's Corner. They instantly dropped the average age of the customers by a decade, and their high heels and short dresses immediately made them the center of attention.

As they walked up to us, Jimmy made way for them and got them stools. He brushed up against me and said in a whisper, "Follow my lead." I had no idea what he was up to but knew it couldn't be good.

We stayed at the bar for a few minutes and ordered another round of drinks. The girls had vodka sodas, and they seemed entertained by the dive-bar atmosphere—and by bar-owner Jimmy, who happily obliged my Jimmy's request to explain some of the black-and-white boxing photos on the wall. He put on a bit of a show for us and placed himself squarely in the history of some of the greatest fights of the past half-century. The girls ate it up.

All the while, J.O.B. stared at the girls, first at Allison, then at Rayna, who actually seemed to reciprocate his interest. She kept tossing back her hair as he stared at her and, after a second drink, she gave him a small smile and held his eye contact for the first time.

At one point bar-owner Jimmy signaled my Jimmy to come toward the back area of the bar. Then he ushered the five of us through to a seating area and a corner table that had just opened up. J.O.B. was fully lit by now and fueled by the sexual tension with Rayna. I noticed that he was keeping his left hand in his pocket. At one point he disappeared into the bathroom and came back without his wedding ring on.

Jimmy disappeared and came back with more shots and beers for us and vodka sodas for the women. J.O.B. downed his shot immediately and slammed back his beer in the next five minutes. Then he waved over the waitress, who exchanged a look with Jimmy while J.O.B. ordered another round of drinks over protests from the girls. He also got change for the jukebox. J.O.B. stood behind Rayna while she flipped CDs on the jukebox, and he put his arm around her at one point. She didn't seem to mind and the smile never left her face. It wasn't until they got back that I noticed she was starting to get uncomfortable. J.O.B. got more and more handsy with her, and at one point he leaned into her aggressively and tried to whisper in her ear. She pushed him away, shot Jimmy a look, and signaled to Allison. The two women got up and disappeared into the bathroom.

As soon as they left, J.O.B. started talking about Rayna, the ass that wouldn't quit, the perfect tits. Jimmy got quiet and I just listened and nodded. Then J.O.B. did what Jimmy knew he would. He crossed the line. "What's up with that nose of hers, though? Looks like she went a few rounds with the boxer dude."

Jimmy stared at the table and said nothing. I just shook my head.

"Still, I think I'm going to try to take her home. I think she's into me."

Jimmy lifted his head slowly and met J.O.B.'s eyes. "I think you're right, J.O.B. Allison told me she digs you. You should take her out of here when they get back. It's getting late and you've got a lot of booze in you. You want to make sure you can perform."

"Ha. No issues there, but I think I will." He downed another shot of whiskey.

The women came back to the table and J.O.B. wasted no time. He leaned into Rayna and whispered something in her ear.

Then Rayna pulled away from him quickly, turned to face him. "Come on. We're hanging out. Dance with me."

She took his hand and pulled him out slowly, while he protested, into a cramped alley between the barroom tables and the wall, and she began to move to the rhythm of the sound on the jukebox. "Drive All Night," an old Springsteen tune. Not her sound, but it didn't matter—she could move. Hips and arms and shoulders and legs, dancing in time, a blur of seduction. J.O.B. watched at first but then realized that all eyes were on him and he moved toward her at an angle, with his arms outstretched, beckoning, like he was going to do some kind of a twirl move on her. Instead his hip caught the corner of a table full of drinks and knocked two of them over. A guy shouted. I started to get up to run interference, but Jimmy grabbed my shirttail and pulled me back into my seat, said he'd handle it.

As if on cue, bar-owner Jimmy walked up and exchanged words with Jimmy, and a few seconds later the music changed. This time it was some kind of Cuban salsa, something that made Rayna shriek, and she locked onto Jimmy, who moved past J.O.B., took her hand in his, kissed it, and pulled her tight against him. He spun her around and led her from behind. She knew what to do. They moved together down the alley like it had been built as their stage, then he turned her and came back toward us. The whole bar watched. I looked at J.O.B., who was wiping his jeans of the booze that spilled on him and not even noticing how he had been shamed. I thought maybe it'd be okay for him if he'd just settle down and accept the outcome. But then he turned, and he saw Jimmy and Rayna owning the song and the moment, he saw the crowd clapping and cheering them on, loving the show, and his switch turned to hate. I'd seen that look enough to know it was cancer. I sat back and waited.

By the time Jimmy and Rayna finished the dance, J.O.B. had thrown back another shot and was waiting for them. He moved toward Jimmy, hugged him, and said, "Nicely played. She's a hot little tart, isn't she?"

Jimmy pulled back and smiled and motioned for J.O.B. to take his place. "Sure she is. All for you."

There with the whole bar looking on, J.O.B. grabbed Rayna like a sack of groceries and pulled her toward the table. She went along at first, laughing at him, but then stopped suddenly. "Hey. Chill the fuck out."

J.O.B. got quiet and drew her close. On some level he was conscious that he had a big audience now. Still he couldn't stop. He hooked his arm around her neck and put his mouth to her ear and whispered something. All I could hear was "want" and "now," and then I saw Rayna's face get mean.

"No fucking way. You're married. Go home to your wife and kids." Then she pushed him away, stood up, motioned to her friend, and the two walked quickly out of the bar.

J.O.B. sat back, stunned. "What the fuck was that?"

Someone from another table laughed, and J.O.B.'s face burned red.

Jimmy smiled. "That's called karma, fucknut."

The hair on the back of my neck stood up as I realized what had just happened. Jimmy had orchestrated the whole thing. Somehow he got Rayna and Allison to help him pull it off.

J.O.B. looked at me like a kid trying to get one of his parents to take his side against the other. "Murph, what the fuck?"

I stared back at him for a few seconds, and before I could think about it my mind was made up. "Jimmy's right," I said. "Night's over. By the way, you're fired. Clean out your desk Monday morning. And Jenny sends her regards."

The night was saved, and I had some hope in that moment that just maybe Jimmy Dolan could be saved, too.

FLOGGING MAGGIE

There she is in her glory, sitting in my torn-up La-Z-Boy, wearing nothing but the bra I lent her. Her legs are drawn up sideways so her knees sit just under her chin. She's sipping a strawberry Nesquik—*my* strawberry Nesquik. She always wipes me out of my Nesquik. Says it reminds her of being a little girl and having no stress. Says the fact that I keep it in stock is one of the things that made her fall for me. Her red-brown hair hangs over the deep, scabbed-up gash on her cheek, almost covering it like a picture over a long crack in a wall. I'm looking at her through slits in my eyes. I'm in a bad way, not ready to talk. She takes a gulp and stares at me, letting the pink mustache stay on her upper lip. Is that supposed to make me switch teams?

I know what's coming, the unstoppable force. Those wheels of hers spinning—she's wondering if I'm awake, wondering when the action will begin. She expects me to go to Atlantic City with her. She expects that once there, I'll get carried away by the occasion, the spectacle of the night and her reunion with Damien and her performance in front of the crowd. And we'll kiss in front of everyone. No tongue but our mouths open, we'll linger. We'll leave them wondering. We won't care. Then we'll disappear into an elevator to a bed we'll share. We'll spend the night together. We'll discover each other.

Maybe she's right. I don't know. I don't know much of anything with this hangover. My mouth tastes like an ashtray smells. Nausea erupts in my gut and pushes up my throat. Feels like someone pounded a skewer through my temple. I see now that Maggie is smoking a fat joint and has filled up my little apartment with its stink. I look at the neon numbers 9:43 on the clock radio, and I want to pick it up and bean it at Maggie's head.

She smiles at me. "Hello, love. How's the head?" Her London-Irish accent peeks out. Her crooked smile tells me she's going to mess with me, her favorite hobby. You tease the ones you love, and Maggie says she loves me. But she really just wants to screw me, or do whatever it is that girls do to each other. I've told her no but I haven't said no, *never*. She's fun and sexy and mysterious and sings like her voice was meant to fill stadiums, and I'm glad to have her off the road and back in my company. And I can't seem to find a guy who makes me feel half as good as she does. All that makes me wonder if I might let her do it. For a millisecond I wonder if she tried anything on me last night, but no. She wouldn't.

"Hey, Jen. Question for you—where'd you park?" she says. I'm hit with panic. I've got no clue where my car is.

Maggie throws her legs down and apart, as if to make room for the cackling that starts to come out of her. I can see clearly between her legs now. Can't keep from looking. No thong. No hair. Bare lips pursed open between her legs like a nether mouth that's laughing at me, too.

"You need some Miracle-Gro for your frontal lobe," she says.

"Huh?"

"You see, miss, I'm a year older than you. My frontal lobe is bigger, more developed than yours. I'm in touch with death. That's why I did my best to take your keys away last night. But you're a strong little slut when you're drunk." She kicks herself off my chair and begins to dress. "Get up," she says. "We're going to Atlantic City. Just got a call from Damien. He got us a comp room at the Borgata. It's going to be legendary."

On the way out, the big Christmas tree in the lobby of my building makes me feel dirty, with its white taffeta angel crowned by the paper-clip halo made by someone's child.

We go out into the cold December air. Maggie tells me not to worry. She walks with purpose, Nesquik in one hand, burning spliff in the other. I'm not sure I can be in a car with her for the next four hours. Where is the car? Maggie seems unbothered. "I don't know if Atlantic City is such a good idea for me," I say. "I might need some detox after we find the car." My thoughts keep breaking up like lines on an old Etch A Sketch. I'm trying to calm myself down. I'm lying. I'm pretending. I know we're going, assuming I didn't kill someone last night or total my car.

"You're pissing on my buzz," she says. "We'll find it. And then it will take us both to Atlantic City."

She's right. We round the corner of W Street and Maggie turns right into the driveway of a big apartment building. I know the building. Sophomore year, all alone, no boyfriend to protect me, and Maggie dropped out of school to go out on tour with Damien. A serial rapist struck twice by crawling through windows on the first floor of this building. I hate this fucking building, a constant reminder that I lived alone and unprotected. I had nightmares of him coming through my window and tearing off my clothes at knife point. Told my dad about it and he told me to get a dog. A *dog*! Big prison-looking building, post-Vatican-II-parish-church style. Parking gate smashed clean off its hinges and my little Ford jammed in between two other cars, diagonally.

I'm calming down. Maggie's plan seems inevitable now. Of course we're going. We've got to go, especially with Damien playing the Borgata and inviting Maggie to share the stage. Especially after the night we'd just had. After I saw Dirk out with another girl, I got fall-down, punch-throwing drunk. Became a mission. Over a lacrosse asshole who told me the first night we met that he thought Africa was a great country. I asked him if he meant South Africa and he said, no—Africa, the *country* where the African-Americans come from. He was reading James Baldwin at the time for one of his classes, and he fell in love with all the black anger, anti-establishment stuff. I said my favorite country was Europe, but South America was a close second. He agreed that Europe was nice, but said he thought South America had more than one country in it. Then it's more like a planet, I said.

Maggie says she'll drive. I'm asleep before we hit the highway.

Next thing I know, we're stopped someplace and Maggie is staring at me, stroking my hair like a mother waking up her child. For a few seconds I stare back at her, frozen by the hunger in her green eyes and the way her head is tilted to one side, mirroring mine. She's looking for something. It's too intense. I turn away.

"Come on, babe. Gotta eat," she says. Then she pulls her hand away and she's gone. I stumble out of the car behind her. The sun feels like a flashlight in my eyes, and the cold air whips against my face. I realize where we are: the Chesapeake House, the last rest stop before the bridge, less than two hours from Atlantic City. On the way inside I think about Maggie driving all this way and letting me sleep it off. She's ten times tougher than any guy I've known, hard often to the point of nasty. But she's also got this beauty that comes out when you least expect it, like a fresh rose petal on a city sidewalk. Like her singing voice. The voice she's convinced will launch her into some kind of proper music career. The voice that got her a personal invitation from Shane MacGowan last Christmas to come sing with him in Dublin.

I thank her for letting me sleep but she waves me away. "You thank me, but I thank *God*," she says. "I was just sick of your bullshit. What should we eat?"

We agree on Burger King. A Salvation Army bell ringer greets us at the main entrance, along with a swirl of overweight tourists, truck drivers, and retirees. At the edge of the food court, a black teenager in a hoodie is putting on a show for his friends. Maggie slows down and points him out to me. He's attracted a small crowd. Can't be good. The teen's eyes dart everywhere. His feet never stop, and his hands shake to a song in his head. He's hopped up on something potent. We get closer, and I see that he's harassing a security guard sitting in the next booth. Wants the guy to look at the words on his sweatshirt, the big white letters on black cloth: "Fuck the Police." The rent-a-cop keeps his head down, keeps chewing his food. I see the redness in his ears, the sweat dripping down the side of his face, the way he refuses to move his head in anything but a vertical motion. He looks more than bothered. He looks scared. The teenager's three friends are laughing and pounding the table.

"Classy crowd we got here," Maggie says, loud enough for them to hear. But the teens either don't hear or they ignore her. "We're definitely eating here instead of the car. Need to soak up this ambience."

Whoppers and fries and onion rings and Pepsi to settle our

stomachs, tastes like a dream. For a while we eat in silence. Halfway through my Whopper, I look up and catch Maggie staring at me again. I look away and ask her to break down the events of the previous night for me.

"What's the last thing you remember?" she says.

"Sitting at the bar, ordering a double martini."

"So you don't remember slapping your man's friend in the face and calling her a whore and a cunt?" Maggie's accent, partly an inheritance from her Irish parents and partly a result of living the first ten years of her life in London, has been worn away by twelve years of living in the States below the Mason-Dixon line, but it creeps out sometimes when she's drunk, and she sometimes uses the old words and phrases like "feck" and "shite" and "your one" and "your man." In this case, "your man" refers to Dirk, my ex.

"Well," she says. "The manager there comes over and asks us to leave and lays hands on you. I grab his balls and squeeze them until he almost passes out. I tell that little fat fucker that we just got a round of drinks and we intend to finish it. I tell him we'll be no trouble if he can just keep the Whore Cunt away from us."

"You really did that?" I stuff a fistful of fries in my mouth. "And then what happened?"

"Well, I look around that bar and see that the whole place is staring at us. So I lift up my shirt and give them a good look. You should have seen the look on your man's face when I did *that*."

Now I'm pretty sure Maggie is messing with me. But not positive. I grab more fries. She says nothing and eats her food. She can tell I'm anxious, and we go on eating in silence.

"Ah, no—I'm just fucking with your head, babe. None of it happened. You saw your man there with the new girl, and you did the right thing. Left your drink there on the bar and headed for the door. Very dignified and ladylike. We didn't pay the tab, but you left your card so it's no problem. You did drive home, though, which is worse than any of that other stuff."

Before I can respond, some kind of janitor kid comes over to show us his new pair of sneakers. Something isn't right. He's dragging one foot behind him and has some kind of braces on his legs. "Ch-ch-check out m-m-my new shoes," he says. His head bobs up and down when he talks, as if he's trying to shake out the words. A foam-mesh Burger King hat sits way too high on his head, and a huge ketchup stain on his shirt looks like a gunshot wound. But his sneakers *are* gorgeous. Maggie makes a big fuss over them, how nice and white and handsome they are. She nudges me, and I ooh and ahh, too. A grin opens up the kid's face, and he giggles and blushes and thanks us. He says goodbye to us at least four times.

Then he turns with his broom and dustpan and starts walking toward the group of teens who want to Fuck the Police. They're getting ready to leave, but I see that the poor kid will reach them before they're gone. Maggie sees it, too. She doesn't hesitate. She jumps up, runs over, and cuts him off. She leads him by the hand back to our booth. One of the teens looks over and points and says something. Maggie pretends not to notice. She asks the kid how long he's had his new shoes and how he keeps them so clean and who got them for him. When he says his mother got them for him for his birthday, Maggie says, "She must really love you." Then she grabs this kid and gives him a hug. She holds him for what seems like a full minute, looking over his shoulder at the teens the entire time.

All clear now. The teens are leaving.

When Maggie pulls away from the embrace, I see that the kid's eyes are wet. He's not used to this kind of contact. I think about how that poor kid must have shown those goddamned sneakers to a hundred travelers and how nobody gave him the kind of reaction Maggie just did. I think about how it's almost Christmas and how Maggie will spend it: alone. Makes me want to bawl.

Instead I stand up and hug the kid. We pick up our trash and leave the place. Just as we reach my car, I touch Maggie on her shoulder and say, "Hey. That was really nice. What you did back there."

She turns toward me. She looks at me but also through me, her eyes dead. "Whatever," she says, and tosses me the keys. "Your turn to drive."

Out on the highway, I ask her to stay awake and talk to me for a while to fend off my road trance. "Carcolepsy," as Maggie calls it. I ask her about the plan for the night. Will she sing with the band? She says she doesn't know, probably not, now that they've gotten legit and have another girl to do the Christmas song now, since she and Damien broke up. Bullshit. I know plenty of girls can sing the song with him, but nobody sings it like Maggie. I've never seen him use another girl when she's in the audience. Damien is London-Irish like Maggie, but he lived over there until he turned eighteen and never lost his accent. He used to be hardcore in love with Maggie. For a while before Maggie moved in with her girlfriend, she and Damien gigged together.

Maggie owned him. She's the one who convinced him to rename the band Damien Henry and the Charm. I was there that night and will never forget that conversation. It went like this: Maggie told Damien she refused to sing with him anymore unless he changed the name of his band, which was then called the Rogues. He hated being thought of as a Pogues cover band, but that's exactly how people thought of them, because of the name and because they did start out doing a lot of MacGowan songs. When he argued with her that all the good names were taken and he had lived on Rogues Lane in London, giving him a real personal connection to the name, she said it didn't matter. Beside the point. She said that would be like if she started a band and called it Flogging Maggie and ignored that there's another famous band called Flogging Molly. Later that night, after we'd been drinking, Maggie referred to that conversation and declared her feelings for me—sort of. She leaned over and whispered this to me: "Hey, you. If I started a band called Flogging Maggie, you'd need to take up an instrument and be in it with me, because you have me totally whipped, babe. Ha ha. Flogging Maggie, featuring Jen Tierney on the whip." That's what passed for romance with Maggie.

Half an hour from Atlantic City, Maggie has fallen asleep and I'm driving, fighting to stay awake. The painted stripes on the asphalt keep putting me under their spell. My head keeps bobbing down into micro-naps on the straight stretches. At one point, the rumble strip catches my left tire and jars me back awake and I swerve back into my lane. I open my window all the way so the cold air can help keep me awake. Maggie doesn't move.

I let her sleep. I see the cut-up side of her face, now fully exposed. Her head is tilted back against the seatbelt harness so that her hair falls back behind her ear. The gash is long and deep across her cheekbone, scabbed up with raised pink edges and a thin black line of dried blood down the center. It curves around toward her ear as if someone had been trying to cut her face in half and take her ear off.

I remember the night it happened. We'd been drinking at a club downtown, one of those places with ten different rooms that turns into a rave late at night. Maggie's then-girlfriend was with us, and they were fighting as usual. I'd dragged Dirk along, so I had my own problems. I watched the melee develop out of one eye and kept the other one on Dirk. At one point, after a lot of cajoling by the club's manager, who'd seen her at a Charm show in New York, Maggie agreed to sing "Nothing Compares 2 U." The deejay turned the dance music off and introduced her. Nobody knew her. The crowd started making noise, entertaining itself and ignoring Maggie. But then the first sung words came out of her mouth: "It's been seven hours and fifteen days... Since you took your love away..." The place went silent as an empty church and stayed that way. Maggie had them. She nailed every high note, bent the low ones, and gave the song new life. Every guy in the place fell in love with her by the end. When she finished, she disappeared into a crowd of her newest fans. At one point, when her girlfriend wasn't looking, she snuck down into the basement of the club with some guy.

She wasn't gone more than half an hour, and she came back alone. But her girlfriend guessed instantly what had happened. She walked right up to Maggie, ripped open her jacket, stuck her head in and smelled her. Then she took the beer bottle in her right hand and shattered it on Maggie's cheekbone. Maggie began to laugh, and she kept right on laughing, blood running down her face and streaking down her neck and her white shirt. Driving home that night, she told me what happened with the guy. They went outside and blew a couple lines off the dashboard of his pickup truck. Then she let him pull up her skirt and screw her in his backseat. No big deal, she said. A little fun, that's all.

Breakup complete. She moved out of the girl's house the next day and she'd been kind of homeless ever since. She refused to go to the hospital and never got the stitches she probably needed. The scar would be a reminder, she said. I didn't know what she meant, and she wouldn't explain. Maggie would never explain much. For someone so wild, her past didn't add up. She blamed it all on Maggie May, her namesake, from her parents' favorite song. Her main role model, she said.

An hour later we're inside the Borgata. The room is a dream: a wet bar, enormous floor-to-ceiling windows with views of the casino strip and the ocean behind it, a couch and sitting area, and an enormous king-sized bed.

Maggie sheds her clothes and starts jumping on the bed wearing only her bra and underpants. I head for the bottle of Jameson Damien has left for us. I pour two big glasses and sip out of mine while watching Maggie jump higher and higher on that bed, her breasts bouncing as she goes. She looks good. Can't keep her down. Not Maggie Dunne. I stand mesmerized, watching her hair flying, her arm waving ecstatically, the muscles in her thigh tightening up when she lands on the mattress. I think of her back at the rest stop, protecting the kid with the sneakers. I feel a rush of love for her and all of her gorgeous flaws. She sees me watching her but pretends not to notice.

Five minutes later there's a knock at the door, but it opens before I can reach it. The compact form of Damien Henry comes rushing through like a battering ram, and Maggie jumps off the bed, lands in his outstretched arms, and wraps herself around him, her legs corkscrewing his waist. He goes with her momentum and spins her around and around and they hug and kiss, open-mouthed. I'm invisible, but at first I don't mind. I enjoy the show, the flash of lightning between these old lovers. I'm happy for Maggie, and I wonder for a second if that's what love is, or should be. Being happy for someone who has grabbed some bliss on their own terms, even if it's fleeting.

Finally they untangle from each other, and Damien notices me. "And how is this one? Ah, a sight for my eyes. The beautiful Jennifer Tierney. My long lost love." He gives me a big, lingering hug. I've always liked him, and Maggie knows it. I told her more than once she shouldn't have let him go. He's at least fifteen years older than me and always treated me like a princess when we went up to see him play in New York. He looks weathered but still has the dark eyes and the lean, hard-angled face. And the accent. A thought hits me: Is Maggie setting up a threesome with Damien? Huh. Maybe she figures that's the way.

I offer to pour him a drink of Jameson.

"Well. Maybe just a small one. I need to keep my wits about me for the show. Can't be forgetting lyrics, you know. I do have party favors if yous're interested," he says, reaching into the inside pocket of his frayed black suit coat. Two minutes later, he and Maggie are doing lines off the black marble top of the bar, whispering to each other. I don't want the cocaine on top of what I've already had these past twenty-four hours. So I give them space and move over by the windows, where I stand smoking the rest of Maggie's joint and looking at the bright lights of the Atlantic City skyline spread out before me with the ocean behind it.

"Jen, babe, come over here. Damien has something he wants to tell us."

I walk over.

"Right, now that we're properly fixed up, I want you girls to be among the first to know. Sony has sent one of their top scouts to tonight's show. They're close to signing us."

Maggie gives him a big hug and congratulations.

"Wait. There's something else. One of these guys used to come see us play Paddy Reilly's in New York, and he wants to see the Late Great Maggie Dunne work her magic. Been a long time in the desert, love. What do you say?"

Maggie just stands there a few seconds, her mouth open, her arms limp at her sides. "Jesus, Damien, what can I say? Why didn't you tell me? Look at me. I'm a disaster. We were out until four last night, and we drove all day. Will you look at my face? Jesus."

"Eh. Nonsense. Your face is fine. Adds to your stage presence. Don't worry. I was afraid you wouldn't come if you knew in advance. Plus, I didn't know about the bit with you until a few hours ago. It's very last-minute."

She shakes her head. "Well, fuck it. I'm not going to say no."

"Grand. That's grand. You'll kill 'em, like you always do, Maggie. I know it. I've got to go get the boys and get ready. Ten p.m. sharp. Don't be late."

The door shuts behind Damien, and I turn my back on Maggie and walk back over to the bottle of Jameson and fill my glass to the top. I want it to knock me out for good. I stand and drink and stare out at the lights and the blackness of the ocean. Fuck this, I think. That ocean is mine, along with the stuff on the other side. I want to do something great. I want to find my own Damien, or ten of them.

Maggie comes up behind me. I feel the heat of her skin, the feather brush of her breath on my neck. She stands in articulate silence, letting me absorb her. I know what's coming, the unstoppable force. Her hands trace across my shoulders, my arms. Her fingers lace around mine. She turns me, pulls me against her, threads her fingers through the thicket of my hair and brings me to her lips. As we kiss for the first time, I wonder what the night will bring, and what it will take away.

THE DUNNING MAN

Got the first complaint from Alice Williams in D103 about seven months after she moved in. Her upstairs neighbor was throwing these all-night parties, and she didn't want to bother me, she really didn't, but she'd had enough.

...Not regular noise, mind you. That shit is loud—car-crash-in-a-tunnel loud. Other night got so crazy, lasted so long, that Ava gave up, got out of bed, and watched the sun rise over the Atlantic Ocean through the little kitchen window—so pretty, that's the thing we love here, you know.... But this wasn't regular noise. Oh yeah—and the cold-air machine quit on us, Connor, and you got to fix that, too....

I called the property management company to see who owned the unit above her, D203. Belonged to William Jones. I called him, nobody answered. Really didn't need this brain damage. Two of the four units I owned in the complex still sat vacant, leaving me way short every month. I'd been banging my credit card silly to make up the difference but had hit my limit. Most bills I couldn't even think about paying. A pile of IMMEDIATE RESPONSE REQUIRED envelopes sat on my kitchen counter, unopened.

But right now I just needed to keep Alice. I liked her and I thought she liked me—as much as anyone can like the guy who collects the rent. I told her I'd come over and check everything out in person. On the way, I stopped at an electronics shop and bought a white-noise machine. Shopped a long time for the right one, could have gone cheap on her but ended up getting the fancy version that had humpback whales and waterfalls. Shamanic flutes.

When Alice opened the door, she looked haggard. She'd

just come off an eight-hour graveyard shift dealing cards at the Showboat Casino and was still in her work uniform. Her shiny gold bow tie hung around her neck, unclasped, and she'd undone the top buttons of her shirt to cool off. All her troubles shot out of her mouth in a breath of fire: the noise, the heat, the lack of sleep, all of it driving her crazy. Sweat dripped down the side of her face, in spite of the red bandana she'd tied around her head to sop it up. She needed to yell, so I didn't stop her. I stood in the doorway, absorbing her anger. She had to let it all out before she'd invite me in. She always invited me in.

She poured me a cold drink of water and we sat down in her living room, where a breeze coming through open windows cut the heat a bit. The place looked much the same as it did when I'd bought it, fully furnished, off an Italian couple from Philadelphia. I'd given Alice all the furniture when she signed the lease, and she hadn't moved a stick of it. Couch and armchairs still had the fake clear plastic upholstery on them. Two-foot brass replica of Michelangelo's *David* still sat on the side table by the window.

I handed her the white-noise machine and told her that one of these contraptions had saved my life during my first year in Manhattan. Drowned out all the street noise. Then she described her noise problem. Not just loud music, though her upstairs neighbor had plenty of that, complete with thumping dance beats and high-pitched vocals. But her problem also included what she called "love sounds."

I laughed. Couldn't help it. "What do you mean, love sounds?" I asked.

"Connor, they're having relations up there. All night."

"How do you know that?"

"I hear them. Ava can hear them."

Fucked-up for a nine-year-old to hear that, I thought. But I was confused. I owned an identical two-story unit across the quad and I knew the bedrooms were on the second floor. "But you're down here," I said, "and bedrooms are on the second floor of their unit. There's a whole floor between you. I don't get it."

"I'm telling you I can hear them moaning. Grunting. One girl screams when she's finishing. She's the loudest. Someone calls her Mommy and says, '*Fuck me, Mommy, fuck me, Mommy.*' And she says, '*Fuck me, Daddy.*' Like that. Over and over. I can hear them clear as day. They did it four times last night, maybe five. I lost count."

"Wow," I said. Couldn't think of anything else to say.

We were both quiet for a moment. I let it all sink in. I noticed a new flat-screen TV sitting amid stacks of DVDs, looking out of place. The movie on top, *The Night of the Iguana*, reminded me of the first non-landlord conversation I ever had with Alice, right after she moved in. She'd told me she was nuts about old movies, that she'd named her daughter after Ava Gardner. We bonded over *Mogambo*, which had made me fall in love with both Ava Gardner and Grace Kelly when I was about thirteen. In the funhouse mirror of my imagination, they competed for my affection. *Mogambo* was Alice's favorite, too.

"Tell me about the air-conditioning problem," I said.

"Shit's broke. What else you need to know? Gets a little cool downstairs, but it's a furnace in the bedrooms. Finally had to just open all the windows."

I told her I'd fix it right away.

Just then, Ava came home from school. She wore pigtails, a

white shirt, and a long black skirt. She smiled and waved at her mom and me.

"Come here, baby," Alice said. "Look at you. Why you never look in the mirror?"

She pulled the tight hair bands out of Ava's hair and redid them both in about two milliseconds. The quick, sure hands of a blackjack dealer.

"There you go," she said. "Now you're good."

"Thanks, Momma," Ava said. And with that she continued up to her bedroom. A few seconds later I heard the sound of a small dog yelping and whining.

I gave Alice a disappointed-teacher look. She'd been found out. Her lease contained a $150 pet-upcharge clause.

She gave me the first smile I'd seen on her that day. The dimple on one side, the defiant scrunch of her lips, the lack of any trace of self-doubt. She had a certain power over me, and she knew it. I hoped it came from a true place. I hoped she knew we stood on the same side of whatever line divided us from other people.

I turned to leave, but as I was getting ready to go, Alice's fiancé came home. I'd never met him, and I instantly knew he wasn't good enough for Alice and Ava or for anyone else. He gave me a limp handshake and failed to meet my eyes, then he brushed past me to get himself a forty-ounce of Ballantine Ale from the fridge. He took a long sip of it and came back toward me, but I stood in his path.

"Home from work already?" I asked him. He winced. I was the landlord. It was before four o'clock. He had some lame comeback about being between jobs.

Alice stepped between us with a purpose. "You gonna charge

me now for that damn dog, Connor?"

"No. Not yet. Just work with me while I figure out how to fix this noise thing."

She nodded and winked, and it occurred to me just then that Alice might be the closest thing I'd ever had to a female friend.

I left Alice's apartment and walked upstairs to D203, bile rising in my throat. These people sounded rough. Even though the Beachgarden complex sat only a few steps away from the boardwalk and ocean, at the far end of Atlantic City's main strip of casinos, its residents were an unlikely mix of retirees, casino workers, welfare recipients, and bangers. No telling what awaited in D203.

The door to the apartment stood open a crack, but I didn't dare go inside. The smell of dope wafted out into the stairwell. I knocked and instantly heard a vicious-sounding dog. I jumped back three feet, prepared to run.

"What you want?" someone said from inside. "Who is it?"

"Connor Ryan. I own the apartment downstairs. I just wanted to introduce myself."

"Come on in."

"But what about the dog?"

"He tied up. You're okay. You all right."

He sounded almost jovial. I pushed open the door and looked around the room. The voice had come from upstairs, in the bedroom, and I entered on the bottom level. The dog was chained—literally, with a thick steel chain—to the table in the living room. He railed at his restraint and snarled at me, foam spilling over the black rim of his gums. He was a pit bull, the kind that sometimes mauls small children.

"Nice boy," I said, like an idiot. "We're all good. Nice boy."

"Come on up here," the upstairs voice said.

I stopped being terrified long enough to notice my surroundings. The place looked ransacked, like a crime scene. Upside-down chairs lay everywhere, and one of them had been thrown against the living room wall with such force that a leg had punched through the Sheetrock and lodged there, suspending the chair three feet off the ground. Empty bottles of Hennessy and Coke cans were strewn everywhere—on the floor, the chairs, the table. A half-drunk bottle of Cristal was stuck between the cushions of the couch, and a huge, sinister-looking bong with a red bowl, a three-foot-long chamber, and a black mouthpiece sat on the table in front of it. Wisps of smoke rose from the bowl and chamber—it had just been used.

Jesus, I thought, if I ever want to fall off the face of the earth, I know where to find the door. Then I saw why Alice could hear the love sounds: The part of the apartment where the dining room should be had been walled off, creating a downstairs bedroom. I could see an unmade bed through the open door. Clothing and ben linens were strewn all over the floor.

"Where you at?" the voice said. "Come on up."

I jogged up the stairs and followed the sound of his voice to the back bedroom. First thing I saw was a woman's bare ass. Tall and lean, she stood with her back to the door of the bedroom, bent over an ironing board, wearing nothing but a black thong and red lace bra. The steam from the iron curled around her hourglass backside and rose towards the ceiling. She turned and glared at me for a long moment, then went back to ironing. At the far end of the bedroom, a man I knew I recognized stood naked from the waist up in front of a king-sized bed. It took me a few seconds to put it together. William Jones was actually Stryker Jones, whose latest hit song, "I'll Love You for Now," had been wearing out my eardrums. Beside him, a second woman stood wrapped in a white shiny top sheet she used to cover herself up.

"Wassup, Karma Lion? That a stage name or something?" Jones stared at me like he expected an answer, but I couldn't make sense of the question and it must have shown. "Lion your name?"

"Lion?" Then it clicked. "No, it's Ryan, actually. Connor Ryan."

"But that sound good, don't it? Karma Lion. Make a good band name maybe. Or an album title." He took a marker from a drawer and scribbled words directly on his nightstand. "Yeah. So, what you need, Connor Ryan?" He didn't tell me his name—no need.

"Looks like you guys had some fun last night," I said, trying to sound unafraid.

"For sure. If it feels good, do it. That's my motto." He smiled and showed me his gold teeth. "But there's a price, and I'm paying it today." Giggles from the woman beside him.

I nodded. What else could I do? I saw his bloodshot eyes and thought of the bong.

"Let me introduce my guests. Meet Sharon, and this is Rhee," he said, pointing at each of them.

Sharon said hello. The one called Rhee couldn't be bothered to turn around again. She gave me a half wave and kept ironing.

"What can I do for you, Karma Lion?" Stryker said.

"It's Connor Ryan. I wanted to introduce myself and also talk to you about a complaint I got from my tenant directly underneath you. About noise."

What I really wanted to do was get the fuck out of there and go back to Alice.

"Caramel sister? Pretty face?"

"Yeah. Alice."

"You dealing with that?"

"No, of course not. I'm renting my unit to her."

"I'd like to rent my unit to her, too."

"It's not like that."

"Give her a long lease."

"Yeah, okay. See, the thing is she's having some problems with the . . . um. Loud parties."

"Loud parties? She don't like the music?"

"Not just the music. Also the . . . um . . . love sounds."

"Love sounds? You mean fucking? 'Cause what we been doing's fucking."

"Yeah, that's probably it. I imagine. Pretty loud, I hear."

"What can I tell you? Between Rhee downstairs and Sharon here, I don't know what you expect a man to do." He turned. "We made some noise last night, didn't we?" He looked at one woman and then the other. They nodded, and the one called Sharon moved behind him and opened the sheet long enough to flash me. She spread out her arms with a corner of the sheet in each hand, and then she wrapped her arms and the sheet around Stryker, pressing her naked body up against his back. She whispered something in his ear. He turned his head and kissed her.

I'd become invisible. Meeting over. "Uh, maybe I'll come back at a more convenient time."

I left.

I didn't make any progress solving Alice's noise problem that day, but I did arrange for someone to come fix her air conditioner.

One thing at a time.

And I got what seemed like good news: Driving away from the complex, I picked up a message on my cell from my agent. A possible tenant had just resurfaced for one of my vacant units, D106. Short-term but good money.

This lease had been almost two months in the making. Right after I closed on the fourth condo at the Beachgarden, my agent had called and said someone in her office knew a woman looking for a furnished place to rent for the performers in a show playing at the Taj Mahal. She thought it could be a four-month rental at three grand per month, almost four times the going rate. The red flags should have warned me off, but it's no coincidence that green is the color of money and Go. One issue was that the renter refused to personally guarantee the lease, insisting that it go in the name of her company instead. She also refused to put the electric in her own name. Not to worry, my agent said. This woman belongs to a banking family. She's good for it.

Tell me more, I said. The woman, Erika Deitz-Hoffman, was the oldest daughter of Alan Hoffman, founder and chairman of Savoy Bank of Pennsylvania. The Hoffman family needed no introduction. They had one of the largest homes on the boardwalk, complete with some goofy bronze statues of children and dolphins frolicking together. Her son, Christopher "Bucky" Deitz-Hoffman, was "coproducing" the show, along with Donald Trump himself, at Trump's Taj Mahal Casino, one of the last casinos on the strip. Son was nine years old. In a certain lens, the kind slathered in Vaseline, this might be impressive. But I knew people with money did a lot of weird stuff to distract themselves from the abyss, so I didn't think too much of it. Nor did I pay much attention to the description of the show—something about animals and magic. The Milosz Brothers: Untamed Illusions.

I Googled Erika Deitz-Hoffman and a short profile piece popped up from *The Philadelphia Inquirer*, complete with a picture. She looked like an overfed Madonna, a trust-fund chick used to getting exactly what she wanted. Too much makeup, dyed blonde hair, her extra pounds spilling out of a formfitting dress that was all kinds of wrong for her. The piece implied that she was first in line to take over the Savoy banking "empire," but apparently she'd lost that battle and had had to settle for Untamed Illusions. Another red flag ignored. Through her lawyer, she'd originally offered me $1,500 per month with utilities included. I countered with $3,500 plus utilities, silencing her and her lawyer for weeks.

Then this—Erika herself had just called back to say that she'd agree to $3,250 a month if I agreed to her other conditions. She demanded an immediate answer, claiming that she had two other apartments she could grab if it didn't work for me. Since I was only a few blocks away, I told my agent to make the deal, pulled a U-turn, and went back to make sure the place was ready for the new tenants.

When I got back to the parking lot of the Beachgarden, I saw Ava walking her little dog around the complex. She smiled and waved at me as I pulled up, and I waved back. The dog yapped. Some kind of a terrier mutt, with turned-out paws and wire hair and billy goat whiskers about its face. So-ugly-it-was-cute kind of dog. I jumped out of my truck and went over to talk to Ava and pat the dog a little. Just as I reached where she was standing, one of Stryker's houseguests—I thought it was Sharon but it might have been Rhee—rounded the corner of the complex, trying to restrain the pit bull. Ava's little dog went apeshit, the way some small dogs do right before they get chewed up by bigger ones.

I put myself in front of Ava, and the pit bull pulled Stryker's girlfriend ever closer to us, its claws raking against the sidewalk, the muscles of its legs bulging. Ava's little dog yapped and yapped, taunting the pit to come kill it. I started to sweat, and my heart pounded in my ears. The man-eater lunged against its chain less than ten feet away. It panted and pulled, making its way ever closer. Clearly the thin woman holding its leash couldn't handle it. Ava froze and her little dog kept yapping its head off. I told Ava to move away, but she didn't seem to hear me.

Just then, Stryker Jones rounded the stairs behind them and jogged up to us. He grabbed the man-eater's leash and yanked the dog towards him with such force that he spun its body around in midair. Then he landed a knee in the dog's rib cage. It yelped in pain and went quiet.

Stryker wore a bowler hat, pajama bottoms, and a robe that said THE LANESBOROUGH HOTEL LONDON. After he subdued the dog, he turned toward me and Ava and grinned, showing us all of his teeth, including the twenty-four karats in front.

"There you go, Lion," he said. "Don't say I never did anything for you."

I laughed, more because of the passing of danger than anything else.

I turned to Ava and saw that she recognized him. Of course she did. Her mouth hung open, her eyes pinned wide with amazement. She took a breath and gathered herself with sudden poise. I saw Alice in the knowing look that took over her face.

"You're Stryker Jones," she said.

"In the flesh."

He winked and Ava giggled.

Then he was gone, as quickly as he had arrived, dragging the man-eater behind him.

D106, my vacant unit right across from Alice's apartment, looked fine, ready for the new tenants. I'd bought this one from four retired couples, who used it for weekend beach trips from Philadelphia. They'd kept the place tidy. I flushed all the toilets, tested the faucets, and wiped some accumulated dust off the countertops.

Only one problem: The "cold-air machine" in this unit didn't seem to be working either. I turned it on when I got there, and the vents still blew warm air half an hour later, when I was getting ready to leave. Oh, well. These people work with tropical animals. What would they care? It'd help them get in character or whatever they did to prepare for their show. If they called, I'd fix it.

As I drove down Atlantic Avenue, away from the Beachgarden complex, I saw a large billboard advertisement. It featured a giant of a man, riding on top of a big tiger. The words MILOSZ BROTHERS: UNTAMED ILLUSIONS were written in huge block letters below the picture. Then there were the coproducer credits: Donald Trump and Bucky Hoffman, the trust-fund kid. Excellent. Anybody with a billboard had to be good for $3,250 a month, and for a while I stopped worrying about the circus and the heiress.

Stryker went quiet for about a month. More than once during this time I wished for more trouble from Stryker—nothing big, just an excuse to see Alice.

But I had other problems to entertain me. The animal people had moved into D106, as scheduled. The first call about them came in the middle of the day. One of the neighbors whose apartment opened onto the quad shared by the animal people had called the property manager who looked after the common areas. The property manager called me one sunny day to tell me that there was a flood in D106. Huh? I couldn't figure out how a neighbor could tell if a first-floor unit was flooding. Then I realized—the water had spilled into the quad.

"I'll be right over. I'm on it."

Before leaving, I called my agent and told her what had happened. She promised to call Erika Deitz-Hoffman and her agent and try to find some way to get in touch with the tenants.

My cell phone rang five minutes later, and there was a breathless foreign voice on the other end of the line. I couldn't place the accent, but it reminded me of a hacking cough. Sounded like the guy must be from some part of Eastern Europe, the part where they all sound like aliens from some cloud-covered, desolate planet. Wherever he came from apparently didn't have modern plumbing. The flood had him all worked up. I told him to calm down and call me back when he'd hired a translator. Then I got my agent back on the phone and got more information. She sent me a link to the Untamed Illusions Web site, which described the two Milosz brothers as refugees from the Chechen conflict. In what was apparently meant as a sales pitch, the Web site contained a bio of the older one, Ferdinand, who trained and served in Spetsnaz, before the fall of Communism, and "killed many enemies." His combat experience made him "a lover of peace and animals." Ferdinand the Magnificent and his little bro, Ramos the Great.

Howdy, neighbors.

I called the last number that had called me and plowed through the broken English on the other side of the line long enough to tell the guy to meet me at the apartment. I had no idea if he understood me.

When I got to the apartment and rounded the D building to the quad entrance, I saw the water immediately. There was enough to make me worry the damage inside could be serious. The unit had two floors, with no bathrooms on the first floor. The front-door handle had been broken clean off. I knocked twice and let myself into the unit and saw a massive swollen and dripping bubble in the ceiling, right over the front door.

I was so distracted that I didn't register the giant cage in the living room until I was already halfway upstairs. I didn't register it at first because I hadn't believed my eyes—and also because the animal lay there, motionless, sound asleep. All I saw was coiled limbs, striped fur, and muscles. I stepped back to the first floor to see if my mind was playing tricks. No such luck. Definitely a goddamn tiger. Above the blood pumping in my own ears, I could hear it breathing, a sound like air being sucked through a wet straw. I coughed to see if I could make it move, and it picked up its giant head and looked at me sleepily through enormous yellow eyes. I stared into its eyes for a few seconds, lost in the absurdity of it all.

I blocked the wild cat out of my head and went upstairs to survey the damage, which, to my infinite relief, seemed manageable. I found a broken knob on the bathroom faucet, and the handle of the toilet had been broken off in such a way that the water had kept running. Must've been the big guy. I felt like I was on the trail of fucking Sasquatch, only instead of his giant paw prints I was finding damage to fixtures made for ordinary men, not circus freak strongmen ex-commandos. The other difference was that I knew just where this beast slept at night—in my new condo.

The apartment was jungle fucking hot, so at least the cat felt at home. Clearly the cold-air machine wasn't working. Screw it, I thought. Let them sweat.

I called my agent and explained what I'd seen. I demanded all the phone numbers she had for everyone connected to the Hoffman woman. I called every number, and the only one who answered was Hoffman's lawyer—Joseph Sandone. When I got him on the phone, I lost it.

"Do you know what your goddamn clients have done to my property? They've destroyed it. Thousands of dollars worth of damage. Ruined the toilet, the upstairs sink, the ceiling, the rugs, the front door. Smashed it up, flooded it. What the fucking motherfuck are you going to do about it?"

There was a long pause. "Are you finished?" he asked. His accent was pure Philadelphia Italian.

"Yes. What are you going to do about this damage?"

"I'm not going to do anything."

"Are you kidding? You're also late on your rent! Are you fucking kidding me?"

"The air conditioning doesn't work."

"What? You want to talk about the air conditioning? Your client is keeping a wild animal in the apartment. In *my* apartment. In my *fucking* apartment."

"The lease states that all the appliances and the heating and cooling systems must be kept in working order."

"Do you know that your client has a tiger in my apartment?"

"No, I didn't know that. But I do know that the air conditioning isn't working properly."

"You're a fucking asshole. And so is your client."

He laughed the laugh of someone who has grown to enjoy making people unhappy. "That kind of language isn't helpful," he said.

"Pay the fucking rent or I'll shut off the power that you refused to put in your own name. I see your game, but I can play it, too."

"I should remind you that you don't have a certificate of occupancy. I know that for a fact. You go legal on us and you'll end up with a fine and a legal bill and no ability to collect from us. And we will countersue. Trust me."

I hung up the phone, which was wet from the sweat off my hand.

That same night, or the next morning, I should say, since it was after 4:00 A.M., Alice called me in a panic. She was hyperventilating into the phone and trying to talk, but the words wouldn't come. Scared me. Alice the Great, Alice the Rock—hysterical now. I kept telling her to breathe. Don't talk, just breathe. All the while I was thinking the worst—that something had happened to Ava, that she'd been molested by some South Inlet crackhead in that godforsaken neighborhood. Or Ferdinand the Magnificent's wild cat had broken loose and eaten Ava or Ava's pooch.

So when I found out what had Alice so upset, I felt relieved. One of Stryker's boys had beat the piss out of her fiancé. The noise had started early last night, around ten o'clock. Louder than ever. Around midnight, her fiancé had banged on the door of Stryker's apartment and asked them to quiet down. They said they would, but of course they didn't. More people came to party. The music blasted louder and louder, and the dancing and the thumping shook the ceiling with such force they thought it would come down on them. At that point, Alice called the cops. It took them over an hour to show up, and by this point, it was 2:00 A.M. Alice watched and saw the police car pull up out front. The lights were off and they didn't use sirens. Two cops climbed the steps and came back half an hour later laughing. One of them said something about not expecting a happy ending. They spent five minutes with Alice and her fiancé, telling them that Stryker and his crew had agreed to keep it quiet, but they also said that they had every right to have a party if they wanted. One of the cops asked Alice's fiancé if he was drunk, which, as she admitted to me, he was. There was another half an hour of quiet, then the noise started up louder than ever. Alice's fiancé kept on drinking, and around 3:30 he went back upstairs to confront Stryker himself.

Before Alice called me, her fiancé had been deposited at her doorstep, beaten up and left for dead. The ambulance came and rushed him to Atlantic City Medical Center, and she'd called me from outside the emergency room.

I didn't say anything for a few seconds after Alice finished her story. Then I tried to tell her that it would be temporary, that Stryker was on tour in just a few more weeks. Then he'd be off to terrorize some other city, and things would be calm again. But Alice wasn't having it. She knew this would happen. Just knew it. She'd told her fiancé not to go messing with Styker, but he started drinking and yelling. But still those people had no right, she said, no damn right to do what they did. I told her to stay out of it, that I'd call the police and make sure they were taking the whole thing seriously, knowing it'd be a waste of time. Seemed like one of the cops, if not both, had gotten blowjobs from a member of Stryker's harem. No way they'd go after Stryker now unless he shot someone.

By the end of the call, I'd promised to talk to Stryker, and Alice had calmed down a bit. Right before we hung up, she told me that the technician had come and fixed the air conditioner.

"It's nice and cool now," she said. "Thank you, Connor." My name sounded good coming out of her mouth.

I went back to see Stryker, as promised, but first I did my homework. He'd been born William Everett Jones, but his birth name didn't play for long in Baltimore, where he grew up, and where he joined his first gang at age ten. Legend was that he'd earned his original street name, "Sniper," because he used a high-powered rifle with a scope during drive-by shootings. While other bangers sprayed bullets indiscriminately, Jones would patiently aim his long-barreled rifle and rarely miss. When he decided to give up the banging for music, he changed "Sniper" to "Stryker"—probably to avoid conjuring images of Sarajevo. By now he'd sold over twenty million records worldwide. He had a wife but made no secret of his need for "something on the side," as he put it. The women in his videos often pulled double duty as members of his harem, which he modeled after Hugh Hefner's Playboy Bunny farm team.

He had a string of sold-out gigs in New York and New Jersey. Had a huge gambling habit, but had got himself blacklisted at Atlantic City hotels after assaulting a bellboy with a champagne bottle and getting tossed out of the Borgata. So his Beachgarden apartment served as his crash and party pad. The previous occupants of Alice's apartment had also complained of the noise—so much that the owner renting to Stryker threatened to evict him. Stryker responded with a cash offer to buy the place that the owner couldn't resist.

It was half past noon when I got to the Beachgarden. Stryker came to the door in his pajamas. His apartment had been transformed. Everything was in its right place, and the place looked clean. No bong, no bottles. Wall had been patched up. An electronic keyboard sat on a stand in the living room. Looked like he'd been practicing or writing music.

"Hey, Lion. What brings you to my house of fun?"

He knew why I was here. "Well, Stryker, I need to ask you to turn down the volume at your parties. My tenant's fiancé is banged up pretty good. He'll be okay, but he spent the night in the hospital."

He pointed his finger at my face. "That motherfucker got what was coming to him," he said. "Now, I like the little girl with that ugly dog. I see her around the place. She always smiling. Says hello. She's intelligent, and so's her momma." He paused, looked at me for a couple of beats, and then continued. "But that motherfucker she with came in here all drunk and yelling, not knowing what was going, but he damn sure got what was coming. Lucky he's alive."

"Okay. But can't you just keep the noise down? Put yourself in my shoes, in the shoes of my poor tenant."

"I was about to do that, I really was. Fact, I was getting ready to give your tenants some walk-away money, out of respect for you and that little girl. Was gonna give them enough to take a trip and go away till I left this place. But then that motherfucker came and ruined the chance of that."

I saw an opening.

"That would be a great solution. Could you ever see your way clear to do that?"

He shook his head. This part of the conversation had ended.

"I'll tell you what. Sit down." He motioned toward a black leather couch, turned away from me, and moved toward a square coffee table in the middle of the room. He leaned over it, put his hand in its center, and pushed down. I didn't understand what he was doing until it was done. He lifted his hand up and a circular bar slowly rose up, revealing a bottle of Jameson whiskey. "Have a drink with me, Connor," he said.

I couldn't believe he remembered my actual name. My surprise must've shown.

"What? I'm not supposed to be drinking this Irish shit? I'm supposed to have Hennessy or Courvoisier? Ha. Wait till you see me doing my yoga meditation on the beach. Don't be nervous. Sit down. Let me ask you something," he said. "You married?"

"No."

He poured two shots of whiskey and handed me one. "Ever wanted to be?"

"Kind of."

"I want you to tell me about her. But first I want you to drink that whiskey."

He threw back his entire shot, and I did the same. He waited, making it plain that I had to talk.

"She was too good for me."

"Too good *how*?"

"Came from money. Grew up knowing how to act."

"You ain't been to college?"

112

"No. Well, yes. I've been to college. That's where we met."

"So what was the problem?"

I looked at Stryker Jones, really looked at him for the first time. He wore a black T-shirt with small gold letters centered between his pecs: G R A N D. A web of tattoos covered his forearms, which bulged with Popeye muscles. He wore a small black skullcap and a silver cross in his right ear. His eyes locked onto me, like a scope catching me in its crosshairs. For some reason he wanted me to open up, to confess, but how could I? We didn't just come from different backgrounds—we came from different galaxies.

"What about your story? You're married, right?"

"I'll get to that, but you're going first. Just tell me, Connor. Just tell *it*." He poured me another before I could say no. I drank it, mostly just to buy some time. But the first dose of it had started to hit me, and I started to feel like he was inviting me into his world, trying to take me into his confidence, and for some reason, maybe it was all the shit I'd been dealing with lately, I felt like talking.

"She was the oldest of four sisters. A knockout. Her dad was this rich lawyer, made his money off of chasing ambulances. Personal Injury Attorney they call it, but the most injured people in his world were the ones he sued. He was damn good at it and almost never lost a case. I got to know him and the rest of her family. Great people, full of life. She had what her dad called a twinkle in her eye, a certain . . . presence. Magnetic, really. Sometimes I couldn't believe my luck."

"Why you talk about her like she's dead?"

"She is. To me. Or I'm dead to her, more like it. At one point she wanted us to get married, and for a while I did, too. But she also expected me to do certain things, to make something of

113

myself. I felt pressure to live up to a certain ideal she had, and so I applied to law school, the one where her father got his degree. He was a big deal there, donated a ton of money. He wrote me a letter of recommendation. I got accepted, but immediately decided I didn't want to go. She didn't like that and tried hard to persuade me. Her father did, too. Said I could take over his practice. But he also told me something that made more sense to me: 'Follow your bliss.' My bliss wasn't law school."

"So she dumped your ass and you ended up a slumlord. Good move."

"Yeah, guess I've been trying for the past few years to work my way back to her, though I'm sure she's moved on."

"You still love her?"

I had to think about it. It was the first time in a long time that I'd asked myself that question. She used to occupy my every waking thought. I spent months and months mourning our breakup. I used to hear her in every sad song and see her in every curly-haired brunette on the sidewalk. The obsession had faded some now, but she still seemed like the best I might ever have.

"No. Fuck her. And fuck you. Let's talk about something else."

"What's she doing now?"

"Don't know. I think she's an editor or a writer or something. She doesn't need to worry about money."

Stryker seemed to ponder that. "Must be nice," he said. "Let me ask you this: When was the last time you got laid?"

I coughed on a drink of whiskey. "What the fuck kind of question is that?"

Stryker just stared at me, too long, and I started to feel like some perp under a lightbulb spilling his guts to the cops. "Yeah, it's been a while," he finally said. "Well, tell me this. Was the last time with her?"

Goddamn it. But he had me, so I just nodded and threw back the rest of my drink.

"Shit. You know what you need? You need what I call a pussy wipe. You need you a little freak who can make you feel good and strong again and wipe away all that negative bullshit. Clear your head right up. I can help you with that."

I laughed nervously and felt my face getting hotter.

"How about that little piece you rent to on the first floor? I seen the way you look at her. I bet she's a handful, but I wouldn't mind getting a handful of that ass. She's really cute in a crazy-bitch sort of way."

"Alice is a good person, a good mom. And yes, she's very pretty. But I don't think I'm her type." Now I really wanted to change the subject. I reached over and poured us two more whiskeys. "Okay, now you. What's your story?"

He took a big gulp of whiskey as if it was medicine. "I don't know if you've read anything about me, but I've been married for almost twenty years to Florence Waters, who used to call herself Flo-Ride. Flo and me had what you might call a business arrangement. We got together before either of us had much money, and we couldn't get enough of each other. But we were smart enough back then to know how things might play out. Getting married was Flo's idea. She thought it would be great for record sales, kind of like Jay-Z and Beyoncé. When I resisted, she said all the right things. I'll never forget this one conversation we had when she was like, 'Look, I know you're a dog and you're not going to stop sniffing around for strange pussy.' So we had a kind of a don't ask, don't tell thing. And a—what-do-you-call-it? A prenup. We kept our finances separate."

"So I'm guessing she changed her mind and you guys are splitting up?"

"That's right. And she wants to steal half of everything I have now and everything I make. Her career has gone nowhere. She lost her best friend to a car accident. Her mom has cancer. Her life is a mess. She's bitter."

I shook my head. "Can she do that?"

"My lawyer says yes. She'll have the sympathy of the court because of my so-called 'lifestyle.' "

"That's bullshit," I said, and meant it.

"You know what the funny thing is? I still love the bitch. Even after all this, I still love her. I don't want to split up. I'm happy with the way things are—or were."

As I looked at Stryker, I could've sworn that his eyes glistened and his whole tough-guy façade fell away for just a moment. Then he snapped out of it and took another gulp of whiskey.

"Hey," he said. "You renting to those animal-trainer people?"

"Yes."

"You think they'd ever loan me one of them animals—a big tiger cat or something? Just for a night. I'm having a big wrap party, and it would be great to have one of those things to set the mood, you know?"

I thought about that caged killer in the Untamed apartment partying with Stryker and his posse. I had to smile.

"You got his number?"

Without thinking it through, I wrote it down on a piece of paper and gave it to him.

"Thanks. You all right. Let me know if you want some help with that pussy wipe. Best way to clear your head."

The rent on the animal freaks' apartment was almost a month late on a four-month lease. None of my calls got returned, so I harassed my agent until I got the personal cell number of Erika Deitz-Hoffman and started leaving her messages every day. Nothing. One day I called her from a different number, a borrowed cell phone, and she answered.

"Yes, who is this?" she said, in the voice of someone who was just waking up. It was two o'clock in the afternoon.

"Erika, this is Connor Ryan."

"Oh, hello you! I've been meaning to call you! I'm *so* sorry about the delay in the rent payment. My people didn't tell me what was happening until this morning." Her tone actually caught me off guard, all sweetness and light.

"That's okay," I lied. "But can we get it paid?"

"Sure, honey. In fact, why don't you come by the show tonight? I'll have tickets waiting for you at the Taj Mahal. You'll come as my guest. How many do you need?"

"You don't need to do that. Why don't I just meet you beforehand and get the rent that way."

"Nonsense. I'll leave four tickets for you at the box office. It's a great show. See you tonight. Maybe we can even get a drink afterwards." She sounded manic.

"Sure. Maybe."

"Are you married, hon?"

"Uh, no. Look. I'd rather just get the rent from you. I've actually got plans."

"Have it your way. I'll leave the tickets in case you change your mind, but call me just before the show starts and I'll come meet you."

And that's what I did. But it went straight to voice mail. All I wanted was to collect my rent. I was even ready to forget the damage and take it out of the security at the end of the lease, but I needed that fucking rent to stay afloat until this crazy shitstorm passed.

I knew she'd be at the show, and if necessary, I was willing to force some sort of confrontation. I thought that her henchman, Sandone, might be there, but whatever. I was right, she was wrong, plain and simple.

At the appointed time, I drove to the Taj Mahal, parked, and walked around to the entrance of the little theater where the animal people were doing their thing.

I rang her phone again and again on the walk from the car to the casino, and I got voice mail every time. Okay, I thought. More than one way to do this.

I went straight to the box-office window and said I was a guest of the show's producer, Erika Deitz-Hoffman. The girl behind the counter pushed an envelope at me. "She left this for you," she said. "But you can't go in until the intermission. House rules."

Just then an older paunchy guy walked up and asked if he could help. I explained that Erika Deitz-Hoffman expected me. He spoke on his walkie-talkie cell phone and then led me to a table right near the stage, which was filled with enormous animals that seemed prehistoric.

My first thought when I saw them was how unprotected the audience was. If one of these beasts decided to eat someone, there wasn't much to stop them. But then, I supposed, somebody somewhere in this building was surely planning for such a scenario—and carrying a gun to prevent the worst case. Then my eyes adjusted, and I saw that the stage was cordoned off by thin wire that the weird lighting made almost invisible. For some odd reason, I suddenly wondered if Stryker and his posse had caught this show yet.

Looking around, it didn't seem like the show was doing very well. The place was about half full, and there were a lot of kids around the same age as the Hoffman kid. The coproducer. No sign of The Donald, though. Guess he couldn't make it. I searched the small crowd for Erika and saw a group of adults plus one kid seated to my left, atop a little stadium lift in the theater. Two men—whom I took to be Erika's brother and maybe her ex—plus a blonde woman with a worked-on face and too-tight dress. Had to be Erika. And the kid. He looked like that kid that all kids everywhere hate. Smug little smile of entitlement, just waiting to take his bows and soak up the attention of this loser crowd.

The show plodded on, with cheesy jokes and bad magic. The only interesting thing about the whole show was the seediness of it—and the beasts. A huge African lioness and a Siberian tiger and a bunch of tiger cubs who ran in circles and jumped and ate apples out of the trainers' mouths and so forth. And then there was the animal from my apartment—which turned out to be a Bengal tiger. She was the star, and was introduced by Ramos the Great with a lot of fanfare: Jezebel.

I spent most of the show twisting my neck around to catch Erika's eye, trying to arrange for some kind of a meet-up to get the goddamn rent. She ignored me.

After the show, her bratty kid got up there and took ten bows, and Donald Trump appeared by videotape to congratulate himself and the kid and the animal people on an incredible, outstanding show. The Deitz-Hoffman crew sat there looking bored. They must've seen this show about thirty times by now, and it wasn't much good the first time.

Then while I was watching the curtain fall, the Deitz-Hoffman crew disappeared. I turned around just in time to see Erika scurry off. I would've sworn she saw me. After watching that shitty show and seeing the way she bolted, I started to rethink the dynamics of the situation. Maybe she actually didn't have the money. Maybe she didn't have shit. My gut said there were sixty ways to Sunday that crazy bitch could've fucked up the finances or blown the money. She could be completely underwater, lying to her family, lying to me. In which case, I was fucked.

I pursued her but got stopped by a security guard posted at the curtain. After some back and forth that got me nowhere, I saw my man from the door and waved him over. He convinced the guard that all was cool and offered to lead me backstage.

As soon as I got behind the curtain, Erika saw me and shrieked. Overkill shrieked. Batshit shrieked. "Get him! Get him out of here!" she screamed, pointing at me, her hand shaking violently. "Him, *him*! That one—somebody get him—security! Call security! Who let him back here? He's come to attack me! It's the dunning man! He has no right to come after me here. Security, security! Get him!"

My poor geriatric escort, who *was* security, looked around trying to figure out who could be making her screech like this. *Who-the-fuck-is-she-talking-about* was written all over his face.

Then he realized it was me, and he looked at me. He actually shrugged apologetically. Apparently, he'd seen Batshit Girl before.

"What's wrong with you?" I said. "You invited me here. You left tickets for me at the front desk, you goddamn lunatic." At this moment I noticed the people around Erika, the animal people and the roadies, had gathered to watch us. I could tell by the expressions that I'd been shouting. Most of them looked more amused than surprised. One roadie with a shaved head and a Pogue Mahone T-shirt actually smiled and nodded. The old rent-a-cop rested a hand on my shoulder and pulled at me gently, but I stood my ground and looked around at my audience. "Wait. This woman, your *boss*, owes me money. She rented my apartment and hasn't paid me for it. She has enough money to put on this show. Her family owns banks, for God's sake." I looked back at Erika Dietz-Hoffman. "What kind of a person are you?" The bald roadie gave me a thumbs-up on the sly. The old security guard grabbed my arm and started pulling me away. I slowly turned around and followed him as he hurried me out the door, apologizing the whole way.

And that was my last face-to-face encounter with Erika Deitz-Hoffman.

The next day, I shut off the electricity in the apartment. It was a short-lived stand, because her lawyer called that night, threatening to sue and report me to the city. I turned it back on and started coming up with a new plan. This wasn't over yet.

I called my agent and told her what happened. She was sympathetic but a little scared, I could tell. She said it didn't seem like the Deitz-Hoffman woman was playing with a full deck, but her lawyer probably was, which could be a dangerous combination. She counseled me to be careful.

Fuck careful. I gave Erika's agent a blow-by-blow account of what had happened. Had to leave five messages, because her voice mail kept cutting me off. I called Erika's lawyer, Sandone, and was told by the receptionist that he was tied up. I said I'd hold for him. Sandone made me wait five minutes before coming on the line. I blasted him. When I stopped, he was quiet for what seemed like a full minute.

"Well, I'm going to get off the phone with you now. And I suggest you calm down and think about how you want this thing to end."

"Look, I'm the victim here."

"That might be true," Sandone said.

His agreeing with me caught me off guard, and I babbled a "Huh?" or some such worthless comment.

"I'm not saying it is," he went on. "But let's say it is for the sake of this conversation. Doesn't matter."

"Doesn't *matter*? I can't pay the mortgage without rental income and I just got a foreclosure notice. I'd say it really fucking does matter."

"The relevant question is, in this situation, does anyone care about victim and perpetrator, right and wrong? That's the question. And I think you already know the answer."

"Nobody gives a rat's ass."

"You said it."

"Tell me this," I said. "Does this crazy bitch have any money to pay the rent? Is she tapped out of her trust fund or something?"

"Look—I can't spell this out for you. Just don't do anything stupid. Think about who's on the other side of this thing and be smart."

"Is that some kind of threat?"

"No, it's not. You seem like a nice enough kid, and I don't want this to get messy. That's all."

"Okay. Thanks? I guess?"

"Don't thank me. Just think before you make another move."

I did think about it. I thought hard about admitting defeat. Being patient. Playing it cool. Hanging tough. Instead, I shut off the electricity again. Had to do it. Without that rent money, the dominos would fall and I'd lose all of the properties.

Two days later, I woke up to find my truck had a flat tire. I put the spare on and drove it toward a service station. It died half a mile down the road. Had to get it towed. Turned out someone had filled the gas tank with sugar and almost fried the whole engine. The guy at the service station said he'd flush out the fuel system and see if he could save the patient, but no promises.

Fucking hell. What was up with this Rambo shit?

For the cherry on top, Alice called me, panicked again. Her now-ex-fiancé's drinking had gotten out of hand. Could I come by the apartment today, Alice wanted to know. She didn't want to discuss it over the phone, just begged me to come by, A-S-A-fucking-P.

So I did.

When I got there, she walked me over to the side table by the living room window. She opened a drawer, revealing a handgun she'd hidden under some napkins.

"Jesus," I said. "What is that for?"

"He says he's going to confront Stryker and his gang next time he has a party. He's talking crazy. Lost his new job. Been drinking all day, every day. I don't know what to do. I can't have him around here. Can't have him around Ava."

"You need a restraining order."

"Already applied for one, but it takes time. Time I don't have."

"So I guess the noise machine I bought you doesn't help?"

She gave me a withering look. I held her gaze for a moment, surprised at how young and vulnerable she looked. I don't think I'd ever thought about her age before, but I guessed just then that she was younger than me. She had no lines around her brown eyes, and her lips were full and taut.

"Right. Okay. Keep things under control. I don't know what I can do, but let me think about it, Alice. Let me try to come up with something."

I walked over to her and put my hand on her shoulder. She didn't pull away. She was trembling. I pulled her to me and hugged her. She hugged me back and put her head on my shoulder. The feel of her in my arms put a swarm of butterflies in my stomach and made my skin dance.

The next day, things were strangely quiet. The Russians weren't answering their door, Sandone wasn't answering his phone, and Erika had apparently fallen off the face of the earth. I expected either to be served papers or to have the shit kicked out of me at any minute.

I used the unwanted lull to go talk to Stryker. I went to his apartment and saw Alice coming down the stairs as I was going up. She was shaking her head and smiling before she noticed me.

I stared straight at her, locking eyes, trying to read her expression.

"He ain't so bad," she said, looking at me without remorse. "He's crazy, but he ain't all bad. He's smart."

I stared at her eyes and said nothing. It caught me off guard to realize that it bugged me, her being up in Stryker's place.

"I had to talk to him, Connor. This has to stop. We're getting no sleep. I'm worried about what could happen. I'm worried about Ava."

"So what did he say?"

She smiled, looked down, and brushed past me. I turned and watched her go into her apartment and shut the door without looking back.

The door to Stryker's apartment was open and I could hear Chopin playing on his stereo. I didn't recognize the man sitting on the couch. He wore a white dress shirt with a buttoned-down collar, a bowler hat, and horn-rimmed tortoiseshell glasses. He was reading a page from a sheaf of clipped paper, holding the page close to his face, and he looked like a college professor. When he looked up at me and put down the sheaf of papers, I saw that it was Stryker. My surprise must've shown.

"What? You surprised I can read?"

"No. Just never seen you with the glasses."

"Yeah, the bitches love these things," he said, taking them off and putting them next to the sheaf of papers on the table. "Speaking of bitches, your girl Alice was just up in here."

"I know." I didn't like the way her name sounded coming out of Stryker's mouth.

"She's got confidence. I will say that. She kinda hot, too."

I said nothing.

"Why you look at me like that, Lion? Ha-ha. She ain't your girl. Maybe she needs to be my pussy wipe, make me forget about Flo."

"I'm here to ask you one last time to hold down the noise, Stryker. Alice and her daughter can't sleep. Her boyfriend is out of control and might do something stupid. It's a bad situation."

"One last time? And then what?"

"Then nothing. I'll see you." I turned to leave.

"Hold up. Don't go away mad, Lion. I'm just messing. Sit down with me. You want a drink?"

I shook my head, rethinking what I'd thought. I reminded myself that regardless, Alice was a grown woman who didn't owe me anything but rent. And I had bigger problems to deal with. I decided I did want that drink. I poured myself two fingers of Jameson and took a seat across from him.

"Seen this shit?" he asked, reading at his sheaf of papers. "*Hierarchy*. Of *need*." He glared at me as if expecting an apology for something. Then he flipped a few pages, traced a few lines with his pointer finger, and closed it again so I could see the title page and the author's name: Maslow. Sucked air through his teeth and said the title again: "Hierarchy of Need." Shook his head and folded his arms. He was having an argument with the text, which had offended him like a woman would, or a false friend. And he responded to it as if to a breathing person. "Ain't no *damn* hierarchy of need."

"Vaguely remember reading that in school," I said, sipping my whiskey. "Some kind of theory of human need, what makes people happy."

"That's right. Homebase, here, says you need food, safety, love, respect, and big thoughts. But I don't know about all that. I'm reading about how Maslow came up with his theory, and I think his methods are flawed."

"How so?"

He picked up the sheaf of papers and flipped through it until he found the section he wanted. "Listen to what Maslow said: 'The study of crippled, stunted, immature, and unhealthy specimens can yield only a cripple psychology and a cripple philosophy.' Says here that he studied people like Albert Einstein and Frederick Douglass and 'the healthiest one percent of the college population.' I say, Garbage in, garbage out. I ain't nothing like those people."

"Me neither. Why in the hell are you reading this?"

"A song I was writing. Got to reading about some ideas and came across this shit. I been through it, but I'm thinking I got a different 'hierarchy of need.'"

"What's that?"

"I *need* to forget that I'm gonna die. Feel me? Only two things make me do that. Fucking and getting high. I don't need the rest of that shit he talks about."

"What about your music?"

"You right. That's number three."

"You also need food. You need a house."

"True enough, I guess, but I just think about those things as shit you buy with money."

"There's another one," I said. "You need money."

"Nah, fuck that. I make the money so I can smoke, rhyme, and fuck—mostly fuck. Money ain't the need."

"The women that you, you know—fuck. You don't think those women get with you just for your good looks and charming personality, do you?"

"Shit no. No way an ugly street nigger like me get so much pussy without the rhymes and the cash. I know that. But still, money ain't the goal. It's just the—what do you call—the path of least resistance."

"I'm not so sure about that. You've got game. I'll give you that."

"Want to see me in action? Come to my wrap party. Three weeks, right here at my humble home."

"I'll check my calendar."

"Your girl Alice will be here. She already told me."

I put my attention back on getting my money from the animal freaks. Well. Another notice from the bank put my attention back on it. I had a new plan forming in my head, but it depended on Sandone. It meant I had to be nice to him, which was painful. I called and left a message on his voice mail, telling him I had had time to think, and I wanted to work something out.

He called me back within half an hour. I picked my words carefully.

"Look, we both have a problem," I said. "But I think we both need the same thing. You need a happy client who gets what she wants and complies with her lease. Your client needs an air-conditioned apartment. You're being paid to protect her interests, so you need to do your best to get her what she wants. I need my rent money."

He was quiet, and I let the quiet hang. Sandone was good at Chicken, though. He wasn't going to talk first.

"Well," I finally said. "Is that right?"

"Go on," he said. "What do you have in mind?"

"I've got another apartment in the building, and I know for a fact that the air conditioning works there. I think I could work something out where your client could have this apartment if you get current on your lease." I had a three-way switch in mind. I figured I'd let Alice have my place for the duration of the Psychoids' lease. I'd move them into Alice's place, sans the fucking tiger. And I'd sweat it out in the shithole apartment until everything was ready to go back to normal.

More silence. Then he said, "Why can't you just get the air conditioning fixed?"

"Honestly? I can't afford it."

More silence. Then: "Is your other unit furnished?"

Shit, I hadn't thought about furniture.

"The unit will be furnished," I said.

"How do I know the air conditioning works in this other apartment?"

"I knew that question was coming. I'll arrange for you to see for yourself before you pay me. But you'll need to pay me before occupying the apartment."

"That might work. I'll call you back."

He called back in five minutes and we made the arrangement. He'd meet me in forty-eight hours. He'd bring a certified check, as good as cash, and verify that the apartment looked okay and had working air conditioning.

Now I had to get Alice on board. She resisted at first, saying she felt bad about putting me out, but I sold her with the promise of peace and quiet and cool and the hope that it might keep her ex from killing or getting killed. All I had to do was promise her that her furniture would be taken care of. I didn't think for a second that it would be, but I made the promise anyway, hoping that I wouldn't have to replace every single fucking piece. As I was walking away from her door, she stopped me and asked if I was going to Stryker's wrap party. When I said yes, she smiled and said, "Maybe I'll see you there."

I needed another day to get all the city permits in order. This time, I wasn't taking any chances. I applied for new Certificates of Occupancy, I had the lease reworked to forbid pets of any kind, I packed a few bags of my own, and hired a couple guys to help speed up the moves. Everything happened right on schedule, without a hitch.

All was quiet for about a week after the apartment switch. I stayed in touch with Alice to make sure the new location was working out for her, which it seemed to be, and I didn't hear any complaints from Sandone. I supposed I had the worst of it. It was hot as balls in the trashed apartment and my exploding sinuses told me mildew was growing in the carpet, but I was willing to sweat and go mooch off Starbucks' wireless for a couple months if it meant getting peace, quiet, and paid. When I finally got a check—not what they owed me, but at least it covered the first month's rent—I actually started to think that was the end of it.

But then I got a call from Ramos the Great. He told me in his broken English that the noise was unbearable, that very bad things were happening and Ferdinand the Magnificent was at his wit's end.

Turned out that Stryker's partying had become frenzied as he finished up his stay. Even from my sauna across the complex, I could tell he'd amped it up. Booze, women, dope, the works. The house-party music was so loud that Ferdinand the Magnificent was going to hurt someone, Ramos was sure of it. He said the music made the wild cat howl and scratch at its cage until its claws bled. Yes. They'd brought the fucking tiger with them, a fact that actually voided the new lease. Also a fact that I decided not to bring up because I still needed the $3,250 times three that I'd get paid if they stayed out their lease.

"You don't know, Mister," Ramos said. "Ferdinand is killer. Ferdinand kill more Russians than anyone in Chechen army."

I told him I didn't doubt it for one second.

"And this Stryker Jones, he wants Jezebel. Every time we see him, he asks about Jezebel. He promised to keep quiet if we give him Jezebel for one night."

"So let him have her."

"Give him Jezebel? No way Ferdinand will never…"

"Look, it's just one night." I was trying to reason with a guy who may have been half crazy and seemed to understand only half of what I said. I tried to tell him that Stryker wanted the tiger for one last party, that he was leaving soon, blah blah. I don't know what he understood, but he hung up, I didn't hear from Sandone, and I didn't read about anything particularly crazy in the news the next day, so I figured everything was okay. I just needed to hold everything together for one more week and get through Stryker's wrap party.

Stryker's apartment couldn't contain his final bow at the Beachgarden apartments. There was a DJ set up near the pool, there was an open bar, and a huge barbecue fired up in the quad. Residents and visitors alike had been invited and were out swimming, dancing, and drinking, enjoying the show.

I left my sweat lodge and made my way to the party's heart in D203. I walked through the open door of Stryker's apartment, and seconds later I was afraid for my life. Jezebel seemed to be floating above the floor, and she roared at me so loudly as I walked through the door that I dropped to the floor with my hands over my face, expecting to die. I stayed down, eyes shut, feeling like I'd walked into a trap. Gradually, I realized a dozen people were laughing at me. "Nice, Connor," I thought. "Have some self-respect."

I stood up and straightened my shirt. I looked around the place, my eyes adjusting to the artificial lighting that I now recognized from the Untamed Illusions show. Jezebel paced back and forth in a wire-mesh cage that had been hung from the ceiling.

A woman walked up to me holding a silver tray with a pink drink on it. She wore a red bow tie wrapped around a tuxedo shirt that ended above her belly button, a black leather miniskirt, and stiletto heels. "Mr. Ryan," she said. "Welcome. Stryker would like you to have this."

"What is it?"

She handed it to me, smiling. "It's a drink Mr. Jones invented called Terminal Velocity. Enjoy."

I took a sip, warily, and looked around again. I saw Ramos standing guard behind Jezebel. He wore his Untamed outfit, complete with a whip, leather dungarees, and a matching vest. With his curly mustache, he looked like a cross between Crocodile Dundee and Captain Kangaroo. He seemed nervous. I walked up to him and said hello. On the way the buzzing in my head quieted enough so I could tune further into my surroundings. Some kind of classical music blared from Stryker's sound system, mixing with the dance music from outside.

"Jezebel likes Chopin," Ramos said, as if reading my thoughts. "It make her calm."

"So you decided to loan her out after all," I said.

"On condition he leave, yes."

"What about your gigantoid brother?"

"Ferdinand busy. He had to leave town," Ramos said unconvincingly. I could tell something was up, or I should have been able to, but surrounded by so much craziness already, it just didn't register.

I scanned the party looking for Stryker. I finally spotted him across the room talking to what seemed to be an especially attractive member of his harem—no, wait. Alice! She looked unbelievable in a formfitting red dress, cut below her knees. And she seemed to be happy. I was both glad and irritated. I couldn't bring myself to go over to the two of them, so I grabbed another Terminal Velocity from the nearest tray, skirted the edge of the crowd, and made my way back toward the door.

Just as I got outside, a strong grip took me by the shoulder and turned me around. Stryker. I hadn't noticed when I saw him with Alice, but he definitely had his game on. Bowler hat. Grill. Tight Tapout T-shirt showing off his tats and wiry muscles. He definitely didn't look like a guy you'd want to fuck with, but at that second, right after seeing him with Alice, with a little nudge, I probably would have.

Except that he was smiling. "Karma Lion!" he said. He was glad to see me. He tied a friendly arm around my neck. "Hey, man, you see her?"

"Who?" I knew who, but I was still in between irritated and

understanding what was going on.

"Who the hell you think?" He extended his arm right under my nose, drawing a line straight to Alice, standing across the room chatting with some Johnny-Come-Lately.

"Oh, yeah. I saw you guys talking."

"She's yours. Tonight."

"What do you mean?"

"I set you up, motherfucker."

"What do you mean, you set me up?"

"You both need a rebound. She's all worried about her job and shitty ex, and you all jacked up about making this money and payments, and blah blah blah. Well, fuck all that and tell me—what do you really need?"

I stood there looking across the room at her.

"And she likes you, Lion."

"You can read that from here?"

"Nah, I asked her. I told you before that I talked to her. And you came up in our conversation."

"Bullshit."

"Well, I brought it up. You don't believe? You want me to holler across the room and ask her?"

"Fuck no." I tossed back the rest of my Terminal Velocity. "I just thought that maybe you and her—"

"You think too damn much. I got your back, Lion, because I know that if I need it, you've got mine. I can read that." He held up his own glass to me. "You ain't got much game, but you got soul."

Stunned, I grabbed one more Terminal Velocity from a passing tray and tipped it back. A minute later, I'd made my way across the room. Alice noticed me close and the Johnny-Come she was talking to was Johnny-Gone. I could tell Stryker had been straight with me.

"Hey, Connor Ryan," she said, smiling. "I ain't heard from you all week."

"Yeah, it's been . . . a weird time lately. But, um, wow. You look . . ."

"You can say it." Her smile was killer. "Won't embarrass me."

"Beautiful," I said.

"Thank you, Karma Lion. That's what Stryker calls you."

"I don't know that you want to be around the Karma that I may have coming."

She leaned in and kissed me on the cheek. I thought I might faint. She smelled like lavender and roses. "You been doing fine by me," she said.

I took Alice by the arm and moved toward Stryker's balcony, getting us two more drinks on the way. We looked out at the boardwalk and the ocean and the night sky lit up by the casino lights. Seagulls screamed in the distance. I thought about taking Alice's hand and just leaving, getting out before the party got too crazy.

But then, just like that, it was too late, and it was too crazy.

A huge man, dressed in black, his face covered by a black ski mask, entered Stryker's apartment through the front door. He punched some unlucky guest and threw another out the door. People scattered in every direction they could, outside, upstairs, across the room. The giant grabbed a chair, moved it under Jezebel's cage, stood on it, and unlocked the cage. What had been just crazy two seconds before went apeshit. Screams. Overturned furniture. People falling all over each other. I managed to move

Alice to the side of the commotion. I had her shielded between me and the wall.

The masked giant put a collar around the tiger's neck and led her out of the cage. Suddenly, Ramos was on the masked giant's back. Amid all the crazy, I thought how utterly fuck-all stupid it was to attack the guy holding the tiger's leash.

Then it got worse. Apparently, one of the fleeing party guests had gone upstairs and opened the wrong bedroom door. Stryker's pit bull came clambering down the steps, barking its head off. It hesitated for a second, but then lunged at Jezebel and landed on the tiger's back. It was over in seconds. Jezebel rolled over, threw the dog off her back, pounced on it, pinned it down, and ripped open its neck. The dog struggled for a second or two, then went limp.

I saw an opening. Amid the screaming, I took Alice's hand and led her into the kitchen. I knew the floor plan of this apartment. The commotion had moved to the center of the room, but the kitchen's other entrance came out by the front door. We skirted two kegs of beer in the middle of the kitchen and bolted through the front door, just ahead of the throng.

I thought we were safely away from the chaos when we heard the gunshots, muffled but still loud, and seconds later, Ferdinand hobbled, his ski mask was gone and his hair was sticking straight up. From the looks of it he'd been shot in the leg. He moved with purpose. He had Jezebel on the leash and was trying to calm her down. She was snarling and rearing up on her hind legs, blood dripping from her mouth.

Then Stryker came out of the apartment behind them, pumping a sawed-off shotgun. He raised it and aimed in the general direction of Ferdinand and Jezebel. Jezebel went crazy when she saw him and began pulling Ferdinand toward Styker.

Suddenly piercing screams climbed over all other noise. A woman came running from Alice's old apartment into the quad, waving her arms wildly. "No, no, no! Ferdinand, *nooo!*" It took me a minute to recognize her. Erika Deitz-Hoffman. Was she staying with the crazoid animal freaks?

Everyone, including Stryker, froze where they stood, dazed and disoriented by the screaming. Then Jezebel reared up and turned around and lunged toward the woman. Ferdinand threw his entire body on the tiger and tackled it. He managed to subdue the beast.

Meanwhile, while everyone was mesmerized by Ferdinand's struggle with the tiger, Ramos emerged from the apartment and hit Stryker from behind with a bottle of Cristal. Stryker collapsed amid a $250 spray of champagne. Ramos picked up the shotgun and smashed it against Stryker's face.

"Stay here," I told Alice, trying to push her toward the fenced-in pool area. I got up a head of steam and hit Ramos with my shoulder, as hard as I could. He slammed into the doorjamb, dropped the shotgun, and lunged back in my direction. I ducked his wild swing, scrambled, and picked up the shotgun. I aimed it at his head and told him to back the fucking fuck off.

Then Ferdinand lost Jezebel.

I knew because an already unbelievably loud scene got louder. The tiger had Ferdinand in its mouth, carrying the huge Chechen by the thigh. I didn't really think about it. I just shot the tiger in the neck. I kept pumping and shooting until I was out of shells and the tiger was dead. I don't know which came first.

Believe it or not, fucking Ferdinand began screaming at me and crying over the goddamn tiger.

I saw that people were tending to Stryker, so I went to Alice. She kissed me like I was her hero or something. That feeling of her in my arms again. Nothing else mattered.

Within an hour the sun was coming up and every cop in the city was there. Police milled about the crime scene all morning, drinking coffee and talking about what had happened. Alice and I overheard enough to know that Stryker would make it. He'd been beaten to hell, but he'd live again. Then we saw him getting carried out on a stretcher. One of his eyes was swollen shut, and his shirt was covered in blood. As they carried him out, he waved and grinned, showing a gap where one of his gold teeth had been. Reporters saw the whole thing. Photographer's flashbulbs lit up the quad as he passed by on the stretcher, mugging for the cameras. That grin said it all. That's the picture that showed up in every newspaper in the country the next morning. Two weeks later Stryker's hit single "I'll Love You for Now" charted to number one and gave him his fourth platinum album.

About Kevin Fortuna

The author lives in Cold Spring, New York. He obtained a Bachelors degree in English Literature from Georgetown University, where he graduated summa cum laude. He is the recipient of a Lannan Literary Fellowship, the Quicksall Medal for Writing, a Fellowship in Fiction at the Prague Summer Writers Workshop and a Full Fellowship in Fiction at the University of New Orleans, where he received his MFA.

Made in the USA
San Bernardino, CA
14 October 2014